THE CAGE

DANIELLE BANNISTER

THE
CAGE

DANIELLE
BANNISTER

CITY OWL
PRESS

THE CAGE
The Captive, Book 1
By: Danielle Bannister

CITY OWL PRESS
www.cityowlpress.com

Cover Design by MiblArt. All stock photos licensed appropriately.

Edited by Danielle DeVor.

For information on subsidiary rights, please contact the publisher at info@cityowlpress.com.

Print Edition ISBN: 978-1-64898-359-7

Digital Edition ISBN: 978-1-64898-360-3

Printed in the United States of America

ALSO BY DANIELLE BANNISTER

THE ROMANCES

The Sweeter Side

The ABCs of Dee

Doppelganger

Must Love Coffee

Taking Stock

What Moons Do (YA)

Waiting in the Wings

Waiting on the Words

The Sexier Side

The First 100 Kisses

The Second 100 Kisses

Where You Left Me-Vol. 1-5

Arranged Vows Seasons 1 and 2

FANTASY AND PARANORMAL

The Hallowed Realms Trilogy with Amy Miles

The Lurkers Within: A Havenwood Falls Novella

The Twin Flames Trilogy

DARK ROMANCE AND THRILLER

Girl On Fire

The Cage

The Safehouse
The Sanctuary

PRAISE FOR DANIELLE BANNISTER

"Bannister weaved a gripping tale with an original concept making *Pulled* a very enjoyable read. I was never quite sure where the author would direct her characters, what the outcome would be which I really liked. And the final outcome was certainly not what I expected, so bravo!"
— *Two Nerds with Words*

"Reading books from authors that you have read before and you think you know their style of writing, and then BAM!!! They go and write something that is completely off the wall for them, you end up loving that author just a little bit more."
— *Kelly's Nerdy Obsession*

"*The ABC's of Dee* was funny and engaging from the first page. I loved being inside Dee's head as she navigated her hilarious dating adventures. She was honest with herself almost to a fault, but her ongoing inner commentary was refreshing and relatable."
— *Avid Reader*

"*The First 100 Kisses* is Bannister's next standalone. I loved every minute of it! The characters are a great match. Complete opposites. The lessons went from sweet to sinful. It was perfect."
— *Two Book Pushers*

"Holy mac and cheese, or should I say burgers and fries *wink* , *The Second 100 Kisses* is just everything to me right now!! A perfect balance of swoon, smexy, comedy, drama, angst, and character building...all while keeping it real. I devoured these books in one sitting and both left me with all the feels."
— *Book Flirts*

To anyone who has suffered at the hands of abuse in any way, may the lock on your cage be easy to pick.

CHAPTER ONE

Amanda

"Shit. Fuck. Piss. *Damn!*"

If the metro made me miss out on landing this apartment, "murderer" might have to be added to my resume under "special skills." I knew it wasn't the driver's fault that there had been traffic —or that I had missed the first bus—but damn it, Universe, I needed a win.

As if in answer, the bus came to a halt, airbrakes squealing at the arrival of my stop.

"Finally." Shoving my way off the bus, I stepped out onto the gum-ridden sidewalk, ignoring the catcalls from the two guys boarding after me. No time for dealing with small dick energy. I had less than two minutes to make it four blocks, in a too-small pencil skirt and shoes that weren't mine.

With no other options, I broke into as much of a run as my stupid outfit allowed. This unit would be rented fast, and tardiness might royally blow my chance of landing a roof over my head, all because I couldn't get my shit together this morning. Jogging down the sidewalk, I tried my best to tuck my white button-up shirt into the only skirt I owned. Snagging this apartment was a long shot at best, and I had to make sure I looked as presentable as possible so that maybe, just maybe, they wouldn't run a credit check.

What? A girl could dream.

So far, I'd toured no less than sixteen apartments trying to find a place to live within my extremely tight budget, and in every application my credit score, or lack thereof, had gotten me booted from consideration. Yeah, I had bad credit, but that didn't mean I was a bad *person*. The kicker was, most of it wasn't even my debt—it was Sam's. He'd stolen my card to buy booze, brought my balance up so high that I couldn't afford the minimum payments, and it had all snowballed from there.

But I was doing something about it. I'd left the asshole behind, was starting over—trying to, at least, if someone would give me a goddamn chance. This apartment was my last hope, quite literally the last listing I could find, and it was, by far, the best I'd seen. The building had one of those fancy rules where you had to fill out an online application before being approved for a showing. I'd been floored when they had called me back the following day with a time slot. This unit was one of those "too good to be true" listings you just knew would end up as a bait-and-switch. They'd present this glorious apartment that had everything you wanted but, shucks darn, it's just been rented! Here's another unit that's only a few hundred dollars a month more.

Still, it could be legit. The apartment was in a new building, as far as I could tell, which meant it might not have much of a reputation as a rental complex. Maybe they were desperate for tenants.

Things had reached the desperate phase. If I didn't sign this lease today, I was going to be on the street—and not metaphorically, either. The only friend I had in this city, who'd been graciously letting me crash on her couch, had moved out this morning, thus, the reason I'd missed my first bus. My couch-surfing days were over, and I was ready to beg and plead, to drop down on my knees and suck the building manager off if I had to. For real. I was that hard up for a place to stay.

About a block away, I slowed my run to a brisk walk, not wanting to be blotchy and out of breath. As I did, I glanced up at the building: Luxx Apartments & Condos. I'd never heard of the developer before, and didn't know why they'd bother trying to put up such nice apartments in this shit part of the city. Maybe the owners didn't know what they were getting into. With their rates, they'd probably go under within a few years, anyway, but I didn't have to stay here forever. Only long enough to lay down some roots, find a job, get my debt sorted—then, maybe, figure out what I was going to do with the rest of my life.

Catching a glimpse of myself in the news-papered windows, I made the rash decision to undo my top button, highlighting my best asset. Time to pull out all the stops. Was it unfair to use my curves to bend people to my will? Maybe. But it beat being homeless.

At the entrance, I straightened my spine and let out a breath, yanking the door open. I paused. From the outside, you'd think the place would be under some major construction, but for the most part, the inside looked finished. Beautiful, even. There were a few ladders out, drop cloths from the paint jobs a couple of burly men were finishing, but there was a lot of new, completed decoration, too. Highbrow. I nearly turned around. This was too expensive, even without all the bells and whistles in place.

Before I could, however, a woman seated at the front desk wearing a tan pantsuit and dark glasses stood up to greet me. Her smile was rehearsed, almost pained, as if one look at me told her everything she needed to know.

"Luxx Apartments & Condos," she recited. "Are you looking to buy?" She peered down her nose at me as I tried to twist my skirt around to the front. It had shifted in the run over to the building. "Or are you in need of directions?"

"Neither. I have an appointment."

She cocked her head slightly. "An appointment? With whom?"

"Uh, I dunno. The text just said to be here now. Or, rather, five minutes ago."

The woman blinked a few times. "And what text might that be?"

"For the rental?"

Another blank stare.

"It was for an ad I saw online. A one-bed, washer-dryer, dishwasher, uh...heat and electric included?"

Her left eyebrow arched. "What site did you see this ad on, if you don't mind my asking?"

Reaching into my bag, I fished around for the screenshot I had taken on my phone, which I couldn't find easily. "Hang on, I have it on my phone." I shuffled around in the bottomless pit of my purse, shoving aside Rita's lipstick, my bus pass, used napkins, and the kitchen sink. I frowned. I needed a better purse, and a better life. "Somewhere."

Still rummaging, I set my bag down on her desk and took out my wallet, which held every cent that I owned, and the only change of clothes I'd managed to pack before bolting from Sam. I shivered.

What if I didn't get this apartment?

"I see it," I sighed. There, at the very bottom, was my pathetic cell. It was one of those pre-paid phones. I had a grand total of twelve minutes left on it. I opened it up, scrolled to find the screenshot, and handed it to her. "There. That one."

"Ah." She didn't take the phone, didn't even look at it. Instead, she gave me a tight smile. "There must have been some mistake. We don't have any units currently for rent, only for sale."

"You didn't even look at it."

"I don't need to. I can assure you, it's a mistake."

I ground my teeth together. "Of course, it is. You know what? I didn't want to live in this dump anyway." I reached down to start gathering up my belongings, shoving the items into my purse with growing frustration. Why was every opportunity closing on me— was I such a horrible person that no one would take a chance on me? I thought I'd made the right choice in leaving an abuser, but it seemed like every time I tried to better my situation, I made it worse.

Just then, the doors opened behind me, and Miss Priss' face lit up.

"Good afternoon." She beamed. "A pleasure to see you, sir."

I frowned. Well, wasn't that a kick in the face? I got a "no room at the inn" dismissal, and the likely wealthy jackass behind me got the gold star treatment. I was so sick of this kind of elitist bullshit.

"Oh, *his* ass you'll kiss, but not mine?" I grumbled. "What, does his shit not stink?" I was livid, sick to death of being treated like a second-class citizen just because I didn't have money. I worked my ass off, but never seemed to be able to climb out of the financial hole I was in.

"My apologies, sir. This woman is clearly in the wrong building."

"I see," he said from behind me. I continued to glare at the receptionist.

"Not to worry, mister," I spat, "The trash is taking itself out." Yanking the strap of my bag over my shoulder, I spun around and nearly slammed into the man behind me. He didn't flinch. I stepped back, shocked at how close he was. The dude *did* look rich, but not in the "I'm retired, and I have a few bucks to blow" kind of way—in the "holy shit, he's loaded" kind of way. He was sexy as hell, too: dirty blond hair that was expertly combed back, gloriously golden skin, deep blue eyes, and a perfectly-manicured beard. I'd never been one for facial hair, but this guy pulled it off.

I frowned. The rich have everything, money and looks. Figures. Even more annoyed, I tried to move around him, but he held his ground.

"Feisty, aren't you?" he asked, as though that pleased him..

My nostrils flared. "You have no idea. Now, kindly get out of my way."

Instead of moving, he took my arm. I tried to pull away, but he held it steady, exhibiting no sign of strain. He was *stupid* strong.

"Patricia, I think you're mistaken. This woman has exactly the right building—she's my 4:00 p.m. showing." He released my arm and gave me a gentle smile, looking down at his watch. "Ms. Jackson, yes? You're late."

I flushed. *This* was the guy I was going to have to fall on bended knee for? Maybe my luck wasn't so crap after all.

"Yes, I am." I did my best to smile apologetically. "I wanted to call to give you a head's up."

"But?" He had one perfectly-groomed eyebrow raised. It was sexy as hell.

"But my cell was nearly dead." It was all I could come up with.

He nodded, giving me a devilish smirk. "Patricia, see that you charge my guest's phone while I show her the unit, would you?"

Patricia sat there, stunned. "Certainly, right away. Ms. Jackson, if you could provide me with your phone, I'll see that it's properly charged for you."

I wasn't going to turn down a free charge, especially since I had no idea where my charger currently was. I handed her my cell, and she offered me a pained nod. Something told me she was going to catch hell for her rudeness.

Good. Serves her right.

My escort held out his elbow, then, as though he wanted me to take it. "Shall we, Ms. Jackson—it is *Ms.*, yes?"

Was he flirting with me? My cheeks heated. "It is. But you can call me Amanda."

"Well, Amanda, right this way." His elbow remained open, but I just stared at it. "This is where you place your hand in the crook of my elbow, so may I escort you to the unit." His voice was butter, husky and warm.

I turned back to gloat at the receptionist, but her head was bowed with embarrassment. Karma's a bitch, lady.

Sliding my hand into his proffered arm, I couldn't help but wonder if fudging my application had been the right move. No landlord wanted to rent out a unit to someone who was currently unemployed, so I'd made up a job. Unethical, sure, but I was desperate—I'd find work. It was one of those catch-22s: you needed an address to put on work applications and W2s, but you couldn't get an apartment without having a job. You almost *had* to lie about one just to get a foot in the door with the other.

"Mr. Brooks," Patricia called out after us. The man beside me, who must be Mr. Brooks, paused, pinching his eyes closed before turning us around. He seemed to grow an entire inch as he faced her, tone clipped with forced pleasantry.

"Yes, Patricia?"

"Um, I believe Ms. Jackson forgot this." She held up the bra that must have slipped out of my bag earlier between two fingers, as if just touching the fabric would give her a venereal disease.

"Ah, yes. Thank you, Patricia." Mr. Brooks let my arm go, striding to retrieve my bra. Patricia looked up at him, nearly quivering with fear—or lust. With a guy like him, it was easy to see why. Brooks seemed the sort to either choke you out and leave you for dead, or spank your ass and leave you begging for more, oozing both danger and sex appeal. Not a good combination for me. He was *exactly* the sort of guy I'd fall for. I made a mental note to stay as far away from him as humanly possible.

No more toxic men for me, thank you very much.

"Now, where were we?" he asked, re-looping my arm.

"For starters, you were going to give me back my bra."

He looked down at the hand that still held it. It wasn't a fancy bra, a basic, boring white one you could get in a two-pack at any big-box. That was the total sum of my bras, too, so I didn't need one getting scooped up by some rando with an undergarment fetish.

"I shall return your 'garment' after the tour."

I raised an eyebrow. "You're keeping my bra hostage to look at an apartment?"

A small smile grew on one side of his face, barely visible, but I caught it. "I suppose I am. I think you'll enjoy this unit, Amanda. It's quite unique."

"I'm sure I will," I agreed as we approached the elevator. I would rent a cardboard box if it kept me off the street tonight, but I certainly didn't need him to know that.

The doors of the elevator opened, and he led me inside. When they closed, it felt like all the had air left the room. I'd never been great in enclosed spaces, so being trapped in a giant metal box with a stranger wasn't ideal. Then again, he was hot. This elevator ride might not be so bad.

This was either going to be the best day ever, or my last one on the planet.

CHAPTER TWO

Connor

What was it about elevators that was so erotic?

I supposed it was the thrill of pressing a woman against the wall, having your way with her before the doors opened and exposed your naked lust to the waiting world. Not that this was the time nor place for such an adventure. Still, my cock twitched at the thought of being caught with my pants at the ankles with this unexpected beauty...not that I'd stop screwing her if we had spectators. This was my building. I could do whatever I wanted.

My lips curled into a smile as imagined myself driving into her, almost able to hear her moans of pleasure as she gripped the handrails, begging me to fill her. She wasn't the first gorgeous woman I'd taken up to the top floor in this particular elevator. I had the timing down to a science. We had thirteen floors to climb, with forty-five seconds before we reached the top. Since I knew the thirteenth floor would have no one coming down, we'd have another three minutes and fifteen seconds before the elevator returned to its spot in the lobby, where the potential for onlookers was the greatest. If I wanted to take her here and now, I could easily get off in four minutes—less if the woman was wearing a skirt with no tights, like this fine ass beside me.

It was almost a challenge.

I could be inside her in as much time as it took me to get hard, which, judging by the slight stiffy I already had, would be about thirty seconds. It would be so easy to yank that short skirt up, pull her wrists over her head, and plow myself into her. One, two, three.

She'd let me, too. I'd noticed how she had assessed me in the lobby—how, even now, she kept giving me the side-eye, hoping to inspect me on the sly. I had that effect on women and worked hard to maintain the type of physique they found attractive. Women loved a man in a suit, but they also loved a bit of a bad boy—hence the beard. They craved someone in charge, even if they'd never admit it. I'd walk into a room, and heads would turn, women and men alike. I was a magnet for desire, and used it to my advantage, even now.

The same couldn't be said for the woman beside me. While there was no denying the fact that she was wildly attractive, her attire was utterly ridiculous: a skirt and shirt both wrinkled beyond recognition, days-old eye makeup, and heels that were more scratches than shoe. Despite her lack of fashion sense, it was clear she rocked an amazing body underneath the cheap clothing. Her breasts pressed tightly against her flimsy button-up. One flick of a finger, and the strain on the button holding her cleavage in place would split apart.

Tempting. I had no doubt we would enjoy such an adventure, but today was not that day. There was a plan, and it needed to be adhered to—there was too much riding on this day playing out exactly as anticipated.

To quiet the beast yearning to come out and play, I knew I needed to lose the semi. One sure way to do that was to conjure up memories of my mother, whose cruel eyes and even colder heart shriveled up all sexual desire. Memories of her always aligned me properly. Despite her harsh parenting, she had taught me well in the ways of discipline. Her method of controlling a situation was what had made me into the millionaire I was today.

She was the one who had taught me failure was never acceptable.

Fucking the redhead in the elevator would be a failure of the master plan. Getting my cock wet could wait—putting her into this unit could not.

I had to focus.

"You must have a lot of applications for this place," Amanda piped up beside me. She was nervous she wouldn't get the apartment. It was cute.

"Several, yes, but I prefer to show potential renters the unit personally," I said. "I'm a good judge of people. I can tell immediately who will abide by the rules, and who will not."

She turned to look at me and crossed her arms over her chest, making her cleavage heave. *Fuck,* she was sexy. "And what does your gut say about me, Mr. Brooks?"

The elevator came to a stop, and the doors opened.

"You seem like the rule-following sort." I gestured for her to exit, both as a courtesy and a test. I wanted to see if she would obey instructions.

She looked at the open doors, then at me, seeming to consider. Sucking in a breath, she made her way out of the elevator.

Good girl.

AMANDA

As I walked out of the elevator, I could smell the fumes from what appeared to be a newly- installed carpet: slightly chemical, with a trace of something floral, and the stench of something dead. That was new construction, for you. The smell of fresh paint mingled with the chemical bouquet, and I hoped it would wear off soon. Strong smells bothered me.

The hallway was narrow with doors on either side. My heels sunk into the deep carpets. That meant they were expensive. The color was a dark burgundy, printed with an ornate pattern that almost looked like handcuffs. I smirked. Someone hadn't been paying attention when they'd picked out that design. Glancing up, I noted dark keypads by each door. Fancy. In fact, the whole place screamed of money. This was going to be an epic waste of time. I was way out of my element, and no blow job was ever going to land me a place here.

"So when's the unit available? The ad didn't say," I asked, trying to find a graceful way to back out of this impending embarrassment. Whatever he said, I could say it wouldn't work for my timing.

"Immediately. Presuming you like it, that is."

Well, shit. I needed it immediately. "That's great. The rent is surprisingly cheap for such a nice building. You sure you didn't leave out a digit in that listing?" I continued, only half-joking.

"Well, the building is still undergoing some renovations, as you can see from the lobby, and the unit itself still needs some work. In a few years the rent may go up, but for now it seemed a fair price." He gestured to the apartments beside us as we walked down the hall. "This floor has remained unrented, as it's still under some light construction. Unfortunately, it's rather loud here at times— again, a factor in the rent. Your unit would be there, at end of the hall."

When we got to the door, Mr. Brooks stood in front of the black panel. A green light came on, running a thin beam across his entire face. A moment later, I heard the door unlock.

"What was that?" I gasped.

He walked over to the door and opened it. "Facial recognition software. Should you agree to the unit, I'll add your facial scan for access. It's quite convenient, and much more secure than an easily-copied or lost key."

"Sure, but isn't that tech expensive?"

"Ridiculously so." He winked. "In my line of work, you have to be the smartest in the room if you want to survive."

Something about the way he said that had me taking a step back.

"I didn't realize property managers were so cut-throat," I said.

He shrugged. "Finding the right person for the right home isn't as easy as you might think. If you can make the right pairing, it's quite lucrative indeed." He opened the door, allowing me to step inside. When I didn't budge, he entered the apartment and waited inside for me to follow. Instead, I stood frozen in the hall.

"You know what?" I managed. "On second thought, this place is a little too posh for me. I'm sorry to have wasted your time."

"Ms. Jackson, aren't you at least curious to see what you'd be giving up?"

I bounced back and forth on my feet. While my gut was telling me to cut my losses and head for the hills, my brain was telling me to at least give the unit a look. He was right. I was curious. Maybe the inside was a shithole. Maybe there was a legit reason the rent was so cheap.

But then again, just because Sam had been an untrustworthy ass, that didn't mean all men were.

I took a step forward, and stopped. "Are you going to try and kill me the second I step foot in the door?" I asked, mostly to judge his reaction.

He smiled. "And stain these brand-new floors? Never."

Okay, maybe I was overthinking this. It was clear he had a sense of humor. Maybe it wasn't a psychopath vibe I was picking up on, but more of a dark wit. I shook my head. That was just like me, instantly thinking the worst of someone. Not everyone in my life was going to hurt me. Not all men were sadistic fucks like my ex. Not every situation was a manipulation of some kind.

Jesus, woman. Get a grip. Squaring my shoulders, I adjusted my skirt again.

"In that case, show me around," I said, stepping over the threshold.

CHAPTER THREE

Connor

Once Amanda was inside the unit, I felt myself relax. The hard part was over. She was inside. The rest would be a cakewalk.

Closing the door behind us, I smiled as I observed her take in the living and dining areas. Each was carefully-staged to be appealing to all tastes. This unit featured an open layout, with the living room to the right, and the kitchen and dining area to the left. But it was the bank of floor-to-ceiling windows that typically drew people like a moth to a flame, compelling them to walk closer and imagine themselves getting used to such a glorious view.

"The glass is tinted, so there's no need for blinds," I said. "You could walk around here naked, and no one would know."

Amanda flushed, quickly turning away so I wouldn't catch it. Too late. It was quite alluring. "Walking around nude really isn't my thing," she said, but she went closer to admire the view anyway. They all did. She surprised me, however, when she stopped several feet from the glass. Most went right up to it to try and touch the sky, but she seemed almost afraid of getting too close.

Interesting.

"You should see the view at night," I said. While she was gazing out the window, I couldn't help but take a look at her ass. "Glorious view."

"I bet," she murmured, unaware of my appraisal.

Her eyes pulled themselves off the windows to examine the rest of the unit. Built-in bookshelves lay bare, ripe with possibility. A long black leather couch sat off the entrance. Beside it sat two freshly-upholstered chairs—one red, one yellow. An oval, brushed-steel coffee table separated the seating area.

I was particularly proud of the dining table. Steel, like the coffee table. Sturdy. Solid. Reliable. It sat six comfortably, which for a one-bedroom unit was, admittedly, overkill. But I loved a large, flat surface to work on. I smiled, watching Amanda's eyes grow like saucers, imagining herself living here.

"Wow," she whispered, taking it all in.

"Stunning, isn't it?"

Instead of answering, she walked back over to the windows, as if willing herself to get closer. Suddenly, she wobbled, and took a shaky step back. I reached out for her, catching her before she could fall. "Are you okay?"

Amanda took a few deep breaths, then steadied herself. "I'm fine. Just not the biggest fan of heights. It's the whole plummeting to my death thing."

She was scared of heights. *How quaint.* "Well, you needn't worry about tripping and falling through. The glass is unbreakable. You could throw a baseball at it, and it wouldn't crack—not unless you possess some supernatural strength I'm unaware of?"

"Sorry, no. The only thing special about me is that I was born on the clearance rack."

I felt myself smile. "Self-deprecating humor. A common mental health crutch."

"Excuse me?" She sounded affronted.

I merely shrugged. No sense beating around the bush when it came to such things. "Nothing to be ashamed of," I said. "It's a coping mechanism borne of past struggles. I'm curious—was it daddy drama that screwed you up? Mommy dearest? Or perhaps a former lover?"

I often found it funny when people spoke to me of their

childhood "traumas." They had no idea what trauma was, or how to thrive because of it. Amanda, however, had an edge to her voice that indicated she might have had a rough childhood. Not as bad as mine, of course, but that was to be expected. Mine was a unique upbringing, one that made me perfectly suited to my line of work.

Amanda blinked at me, as though she'd never had someone speak so directly to her before. She would need to get used to that. There was no time for pleasantries in my profession. When she didn't answer, I continued.

"For me, it was my mother. Vicious woman. Never told me she loved me, seemed highly annoyed that I was even alive—that sort of thing. You learn pretty quickly to either laugh or moan about how unfair life is."

Amanda's eyes were on me, taking in every twitch of my lips. Could that be sympathy? That was a first. Then again, she didn't know the real me yet.

Cocking my head, I gave her a suggestive look up and down. "Tell me, Amanda, are you a moaner?"

The innuendo caused her to flush again. I rather enjoyed being able to summon that color with only a few words.

She shrugged. "Not really the moaning sort. What good does complaining do?"

"Agreed." I smiled. "You have to be tough to survive in this world."

"Yep." Her lips made the "p" pop, echoing off the walls.

"Well, in any event, this is the apartment," I continued. "The bedroom is through there. The bathroom is to the left of that. The kitchen is arguably small, but ideal for someone without a family. I presume it would just be you living here—you don't like to throw raging parties, do you?"

"No ragers, not my scene. I'm new to the area, sort of a loner. You'd hardly know I was here."

With that ass, I'd notice.

She walked into the kitchen, running her delicate fingers over the countertops, a look of disbelief on her face. It was clear that this was far better than what she was used to. "This is a nice unit, but *way* out of my price range." I saw her shoulders slump. "I know an upsell when I see one."

"This isn't an upsell."

"Sure it is." Shaking her head, Amanda headed for the door. "Places like this aren't built for people like me. We don't get the lap of luxury. We get the scraps off the ground." She stood inches from the door, her hand curled around the handle. I held my breath.

Then, she stopped.

"For the record," Amanda said to the door, "it was my father. My mother didn't live long enough for me to remember if she ever said that she loved me. But my dad...well, he made sure I knew that he didn't."

A kindred spirit. I knew there was something special about her. "I am well aware of your financial situation, Ms. Jackson," I said. "That is why you were chosen above all the other applicants."

She turned her head slightly to look at me. "And just how are you aware of my financial situation?"

"Your application."

Her eyes narrowed. "I didn't list my salary on the application."

She was smart. I merely clasped my hands in front of me. "I do my homework on all possible tenants. Thanks to the internet, it's not very hard to hide personal data from people with the means to know where to look. And I have the means." I sat down on the dining table bench, and gestured for her to do the same. "Please, sit. I'd like to discuss the terms—if you're still interested, that is."

"Unless your terms are $750 bucks a month with the amenities listed in the ad, I can't afford this." She let go of the handle and threw her hands up in the air. "Maybe you think I'm playing or something, but I literally have $1,458 to my name. I'm sure your internet search also told you that I don't technically have the waitressing job I claim to have, so unless I can find work fast, I might not even be able to afford next month's rent. But it's impossible to find a job without an address...so I'm fucked no matter what."

Such a dirty mouth. I would have fun breaking her of that. I stood up and walked over to her. Our faces were nearly nose-to-nose, so close that I could smell her desire for me. "Ms. Jackson, why don't you at least read over the lease agreement? If, after reviewing that, you no longer want the unit, I shall bid you farewell —but I think you'll find the offer well within your means."

She raised an eyebrow. "Where's the agreement?"

Like taking candy from a baby. I folded my hands in front of me. "Just there, on the dining room table." Her eyes followed my gaze, to a manila folder sitting in the center of the table.

I leaned down close to her ear, and the scent of aloe washed over me. It was all I could do not to move those red locks away from her neck to inhale more of her, but I restrained myself. "I'll step out in the hall and give you a minute to look it over."

Walking to the door, I opened it and stepped out into the hallway. Hearing the lock click shut, I smiled.

This was too easy.

AMANDA

I'm not sure what Brooks thought looking at a contract would do: I wasn't an attorney, and I was sure the fine print would list one hundred and one ways I'd be screwed over if I took this place. Then again, this was an amazing unit, minus the height. I didn't want to admit it, but I could see myself living in a place like this. That kitchen, while on the small side, would be perfect for me. I wasn't much of a cook, so I didn't need tons of counter space: just a fridge, stove, and microwave, and my needs would be set.

One thought gnawed at me, though. This place was way too nice...and Brooks was way too sexy. Was the contract he wanted me to look at some sort of trade situation—affordable rent for sexual favors? Not that I'd be opposed to that. The guy was seriously hot. If he asked, I'd probably lay down on that dining room table and let him do dirty things to me.

Amanda!

I had to focus. I could *not* fall for another fuckboy. The man was trouble—I'd known it the moment I looked at him—and toxic men were my Achilles' heel. I fell for them every damn time. Hell, a toxic man was the reason I was currently in the mess I was in: broke, homeless, and desperate.

Shaking away thoughts of my drunk and abusive ex, I squared my shoulders. I'd escaped that shit show. I was starting over, even if it meant starting over with little more than the clothes and cash on me. It was still better than where I had been.

I felt the underside of my left breast, making sure the rolled-up bills were still in place. All the money I had in the world—was I going to gamble it all on this? What other choice did I have? I owed it to myself to at least read the contract. Relenting, I picked up the envelope. It was surprisingly light for a lease agreement. Opening it, I peered inside.

It was empty.

"What the hell?" I whispered.

Frowning, I gave the envelope a shake. I looked under the table, thinking maybe it had fallen out, but there was nothing there.

The idiot forgot to leave the contract. Sighing, I walked back over to the entrance.

"Um, there's nothing in the envelope," I called, as I tried to open the door. It didn't work. *Odd.* Yanking on the handle, I tried again, but it still didn't budge. Was it a "push" instead of a "pull?" I gave the door a shove. Nothing.

That was when I noticed a little black rectangle on the handle, almost like the finger scanner I used to have on my laptop before Sam had sold it to buy booze. High-tech security. Of course this place had fingerprint scanners.

"Hey, the door is locked," I said. "Can you open it up?"

For a moment, he didn't answer, and I wondered if he had heard me. I called out again, "Mr. Brooks? The door is locked. Can you open it, please?"

I pressed my ear to the door to listen for any movement. Just then, there was a series of three small beeps, followed by the metallic sound of something sliding into place—almost like a lock. A shiver ran up my spine.

I tried the door again. Nothing.

"Hey, let me out of here!"

"Don't worry, Amanda," Brooks said through the door. "You got the unit. Your basic needs and meals will be provided, so long as you listen and do what I say. I have other business to attend to now, but I'll be back soon. Until then, take a look around. Welcome home, pet."

What. The. Fuck.

CHAPTER FOUR

Connor

It was criminal how effortless it was to convince women like Amanda to take the bait. The cheap rental scheme had been, by far, the best lure I'd used in recent years, and having an application allowed me to properly investigate the women before stealing them. The key factor was to make sure that the women were loners—the last thing I needed was a nosy P.I. or cocky police detective out looking for them. I was hunting for women who wouldn't be missed if they suddenly disappeared. There was an abundant amount of them, especially among the poor, but few turned out to be as luscious as Amanda. She would fetch an obscene price, and I knew just who to sell her to.

A woman like Amanda had the right assets to please any number of my past clients, but there was one I had been keeping a particular eye on: Malcolm Luxx. The former owner of this very apartment complex, Luxx had made me pay through the nose for this building. Pretentious ass. The bastard hated me, always had—as if he thought he was better than me? He worked in the black market just like I did, an "artist" I didn't believe for one second actually painted what he sold. There was no way—why sell on the black market if the paintings were really his? Then again, black-market buyers could afford the price tags Luxx demanded.

I would have thought he would've cut me a deal on the building, since we both walked on the wrong side of the law, but instead the prick had jacked up the cost. It was almost like he'd known I was desperate to get the building—I had acquired a large shipment of pets and needed a place to house them, fast. I'd had no choice but to pay more than twice what the property was worth.

Malcolm really should've known better than to cross me: I knew how to play the long game. One day soon, I'd find a pet that would be irresistible to him, and then he'd pay me whatever I wanted. He'd have to bow down to me and my demands, and I'd make my money back from the sale of the building—and then some. So far, however, he hadn't been tempted by any of the girls I'd shown him. None of the boys, either. That meant he was either asexual, or I hadn't scratched his particular kink yet. My hunch was on the latter. Everyone had a sexual weak spot they'd pay top dollar for, and I was determined to find his.

Ironically, it was the front desk receptionist, Patricia's, master handler that had suggested Malcolm might go for a redhead. My research indicated that his mother was a ginger—hello, Freud—so naturally, when Amanda Jackson and her red locks had shown up in my email as an applicant for the unit, I knew I might have a winner. A quick internet search showed that Amanda was not only gorgeous, with that bee-stung lip all my clients loved, but she had a great body and giant doe eyes to boot. A rare treat. After meeting with her today, I realized how tempted Malcolm might be by her.

Hell, I might need to give her a test run myself.

My crotch twitched thinking about it. Encouraged by the thought of getting my revenge on Malcolm, I pulled out my burner phone and punched in a few numbers, waiting for the tone to record my message.

"Luxx, it's Brooks—long time no chat. Look, I have something you might enjoy. I'll send the deets soon via my usual channels. It still needs to be housebroken, but hey, that's half the fun. I think you'll get a kick out of this one. I'll be in touch."

Just as I was about to ride the elevator back downstairs, I glanced at my watch. I should probably check in on one of my other pets. Her owner would be here to retrieve her tomorrow. I shifted my cock. Might as well get in one last ride while I was there.

I walked over to the scanner next to her unit. The screen came alive once it registered my face, and I tapped through a few feeds to see where she was inside. Not in the living room, or the kitchen. I slid a finger across the screen, pulling up the bedroom.

"Motherfucker," I hissed.

Disengaging the deadbolt, I rushed into the bedroom and cut her dangling body from the ceiling fan. The crazy bitch had fashioned herself a noose from her bedsheets. She fell to the ground with a loud thud. Pressing my ear to her chest, I listened for a pulse. Nothing. Judging by the color of her skin, she'd been dead for a while.

"Fuck," I spat.

Stacey had always been compliant, had always done what she'd been told. It was the only reason I'd allowed her sheets in the first place—she'd earned them for good behavior.

That's what I get for being nice. A failed sale.

Frowning, I cursed again. Not only was the loss of a pet going to cost me money, but it was also going to cost me to dispose of her body. Highly annoying. Digging out my cell, I scrolled through my contacts until I got to the one labeled "Portland Cleaners."

"Yeah, hey, it's Brooks. I need a trash removal. Number 13G. Yes, I know it's extra. Just get it done. I need the unit ready for next week."

I hung up. I could likely stall my buyer for a few days. Scrawny brunettes were easy to come by, and there was even a chance I might find him someone that could pass as Stacey. But there, again —more work.

These fucking women. Why couldn't they do as they were told?

Beyond frustrated, I locked the place back up and went

downstairs to the lobby. Patricia stood as soon as I entered. She'd been trained well.

"Is something the matter, sir?"

"The cleaners will be here soon for a 'trash removal.' See that they're let in without issue." Her face blanched, knowing full well what that meant. "Get your ass into my office. You're going to pay for your blunder earlier."

Her eyes widened as I undid my belt. "But...but I'm Mr. Anderson's pet, now."

"You still work for me," I growled. "And when I tell you to go to my office and get on your knees, that is exactly what you'll do, or you'll get more than my dick in your mouth—you'll get the full power of this belt across your ass."

Patricia flinched. She didn't like my type of belt play. Few did, but that was sort of the point. It motivated them to do exactly what I wanted.

"Yes, Mr. Brooks. Right away." She lowered her gaze and strode into my office, just off the lobby, unlocking the door and planting herself on her knees in front of the desk. There were still a few construction workers fixing the lights out in the lobby, but I'd be damned if they were going to get in the way of my release. I was frustrated by Stacey's selfishness, and surprisingly turned on by the bombshell I'd just caged. I needed to come, and I needed it now. What did I care if these minimum wage workers could see Patricia and I through the windows? Maybe they might learn a thing or two about how to take what they wanted.

I didn't even bother to close the door. "Begin."

"Y-yes, sir," she mumbled. Her eyes flicked first to the open door, then to the windows.

I ripped the belt off my pants and slapped it hard against the floor, making her jump. "*Now*, Patricia."

She gave me no grief after that warning. See? It was easy once they were housebroken. That was when the real fun could begin... and I couldn't wait to play with Amanda. I imagined her red lips sliding over my cock as Patricia sucked me off.

Soon, my pet. Soon, you'll be trained, and we'll have all sorts of fun.

AMANDA

This was some sort of a joke. A prank, or some hidden-camera show. It *had* to be.

Because if it wasn't...

"Hey! This isn't funny. Let me out!" I shouted, kicking the door. I tried the handle again, but it wouldn't budge. There was no crack along the bottom either to try and look under.

This was crazy. He couldn't just lock me in.

I dug into my purse, searching for my phone. "Fuck, that chick took it to 'charge' it. *Shit.*" The other things in my purse weren't useful in any way. "Damn it!"

There had to be another exit, some way of getting out of this place. Obviously, the windows were a no-go. Brooks had said they were unbreakable, but even if they were, I was on the thirteenth floor. No surviving a jump from here.

I did a quick scan of the living room: nothing but a wall of empty bookshelves that stretched up to the ceiling. The kitchen was another dead end. There was nothing in any of the cupboards or drawers, nothing at all that might be used as a weapon. My stomach sank at the realization. This asshole knew what he was doing. He wasn't looking for a tenant—he was opening the door to a cage.

And I had walked right into it.

"No. *No.* There has to be a way out." I stormed into the bedroom, which held a queen mattress on the floor with no sheets, not even a pillow. In the corner, there was a small desk and metal chair, both of which were bolted to the ground. Off the bedroom, there was a small bathroom with a stand-up shower. There were no shower curtains, shampoo, or soap dispensers to be found, let alone towels. Hurrying over to the desk, I yanked open the drawers. They were all empty—not even a pencil or a pad of paper.

"Okay, Amanda. Get a grip. There has to be some explanation for this." I walked back into the living room, trying the door again in vain.

"Let me out of here you son of a bitch! Help! Help! Someone, please, help me!"

"Oh my God, shut up. He's gone."

My ears pricked up. It was a woman's voice. Faint, but definitely there.

"Who is that? Who's speaking?" I spun around the room and didn't see anyone. Was I hallucinating?

"I'm in the unit beside you," the voice replied. "Now, keep it down. I'm trying to sleep."

My eyes flicked to where the sound was coming from. A small vent about the size of my hand ran along the baseboard of the kitchen. I ran over to the vent, and bent down to peer through it. The light was faint, but I could make out a white carpet. An uncovered mattress lay on the floor.

"Please, you have to help me," I said. "You need to call the police. I'm being held here against my will—"

"Yeah, yeah, we all are. No amount of shouting or scratching your nails on the door will change that. You'll be let out when he decides, not before. Now, shut up."

"No! No, please, talk to me. Tell me what's happening. What do you mean *all*? How many are being held here?"

I pressed my face to the vent, trying to capture more of the limited scope of the room next door. The mattress squeaked, and I saw the edge of a bare foot. A second later, the vent on the woman's side closed, followed by the loud thump of what I assumed to be her mattress falling against the opening.

She'd shut me out.

I sat back up and stared at the vent in horror. It wasn't some bizarre mistake that I'd been locked in this unit. I'd been kidnapped.

And even worse, I wasn't alone.

CHAPTER FIVE

Connor

Once I was through with Patricia, I allowed her to stand up. She kept her eyes down, as she'd been trained, waiting for permission to leave. I took my time putting my dick back inside my pants, knowing how uncomfortable she was.

"Do you know why I called you in here, Patricia?"

She shook her head once.

"You nearly cost me a pet today. You tried to send her off. You knew damn well why she was here, but you were trying to save her, weren't you?"

Patricia didn't say anything. She didn't need to. I wasn't stupid.

"Interfere with my work again," I continued, "and I'll be calling the cleaners to your station. This is your only warning. Do you understand?"

Her eyes widened at my threat. Did she honestly think she was the first outdoor pet to try and save the strays from me? Personally, I thought outdoor pets were dangerous. A liability. But there wasn't a way I could force their owners to keep them locked up. That was why outdoor pets had to sign an NDA if they wanted the privilege of leaving their house. Thankfully, my legal name wasn't anywhere near things that could link me to my business.

"Leave me," I ordered. Patricia scrambled out of my office.

Zipping my fly, I adjusted my cock and walked over to my desk. A fingerprint scan unlocked my laptop, and I opened up the new file for Amanda.

"Okay, let's see what dirt Antonio found for me." In my Dropbox was a folder that simply read "Stray 781." I unzipped the file and waited for the data to load. There were the usual findings: eviction notices, parking tickets, bounced-check flags—all things a rational landlord would turn away. Not me. Things like that made for an ideal target, someone desperate enough to respond to the ads I placed. No logical person would want to view a unit in a building like this for such a low price. They'd assume it was either a typo, or a real piece of shit place. But to be safe, and weed out the merely curious, I attached an application through which I could pull basic information on the applicant from their answers.

Along with the expected info, there was also a news article from about six months ago Antonio had found with Amanda's name in it. Clicking open the attachment, I began to read.

SEATTLE MAN TURNS HIMSELF IN FOR ATTEMPTED MURDER OF GIRLFRIEND

Seattle, WA—Seattle native Samuel P. Banner, thirty-one, was arrested late Wednesday night after allegedly trying to strangle his girlfriend of seven years, thirty-one year-old, Amanda Jackson,. Jackson, a waitress, was found lying unconscious in Banner's apartment when authorities arrived on the scene. There was evidence of prior physical abuse, which Jackson denied comment on. Alcohol is believed to have been involved. Banner is currently being held without bail at King County Adult Detention on charges of attempted homicide, and domestic assault.

My lips curled into a sneer. "Bingo."

A fucked-up psyche: that was the key to making a good pet. While it wasn't impossible to break a girl who had never been physically or mentally abused, it took longer. According to this article, Amanda had stayed with her abuser for seven years, meaning her will could be easily broken—and a faster payday for me.

Collecting the necessary specs, I pulled together a new file for Malcolm Luxx. It would be a treat to gather the photos of this new pet for him. My smile widened. I had a good feeling about this one. She was going to bring the elusive bachelor to his knees, and make me an even richer man in the process.

After putting in a new ad for Stacey's soon-to-be-available cage, I powered down my laptop and secured it in the safe. I didn't trust these electricians as far as I could throw them. Though I knew Patricia wouldn't step foot in my office without permission, these day-workers were not under my thumb. The most power I had over them was firing them. With my pets, however, I was the supreme being: they did whatever I wanted, whenever I wanted it. Mother would have been proud—finally, her son had made something of himself. People listened when I spoke. She'd taught me how to dominate the weak at a young age, and I only wished she had lived to see her teachings come to fruition.

Just as I was about to leave for the night, the phone in my office rang. There was only one person who would condescend to call me this late in the day. Sighing, I went back to my desk and leaned on the edge. Picking up the receiver, I ran my hand over my forehead.

"Put him through, Patricia," I spat.

"Right away, sir." There was a click, and then my dad was on the line.

"There's my boy. How are you?" There it was, that nervous tinge to his voice I'd grown to despise.

"Dad, don't be such a pussy," I replied. "Just ask for what you want."

"Now, there's no need to use that language..."

I rolled my eyes. "Are you going to lecture *me* on manners?"

"It's not about manners, son, it's about respecting your elders. When I was your age, I—"

"Yeah, yeah, yeah. How much do you need this time?"

My dad was quiet for a moment. "Can't a father just call his son to check on him?"

My fingers dug through my hair, breaking some strands free from their slicked prison. "A father can, yes, but you never have. How much—a thousand? Two?"

"I need ten," he squeaked.

"Ten *grand*? What the hell for? Jesus, don't tell me you're gambling again?"

"There were really good odds, Connie—"

"Don't call me that," I snapped. My mother had called me that —her way of emasculating me. She knew I hated it, which is why she had kept it up. But I wasn't that little boy anymore, and there was no way a weak-ass man like my father was going to try and control me.

"Sorry, son," my dad continued. "I messed up big this time. This bookie, he's not known for being patient, so..."

I sighed. "You'll have your money in a few hours, but this needs to stop. I won't always be here to bail you out."

"Oh, thank you, Conn—"

I hung up before he could finish. What an absolute waste of space that man was. Weak. Prone to addiction. I refused to be anything like him, never letting anything or anyone close enough to get addicted to. That was the key. I was the master of my body, my mind, and my pets.

Glancing at the clock, I turned back to the safe and pulled out the camera and tripod. Might as well button up this file tonight. All that was missing from Malcolm's dossier were pictures of his prospective new pet.

AMANDA

"Think, Amanda. *Think*."

There had to be a way to get out of here. Since the other

woman wasn't speaking to me, I had to find other viable options. I went back to the door to look for any signs of weakness.

Maybe I could jimmy the pins out of the door hinges? Unfortunately, they were on the outside. A wave of nausea swept over me.

What if Brooks never came back? What if I was going to be left here to die?

That's when I heard the faint ding of the elevator. Hope surged through my veins, and I started pounding hard against the door.

"Help! Help! I'm being held in here against my will. Help! Please, someone, call the police!" I was screaming so loud I felt like my throat was on fire. Only silence greeted me.

"Oh, pet," Brooks said from outside the door. "No one is coming to save you." His voice was calm. Dangerous. "Haven't you figured that out yet? You're mine now—or, at least, mine until I'm done with you. Now, step away from the door. I'm coming inside."

I scanned the room for some sort of weapon. There wasn't anything to be found. I curled my hands into fists, ready to attack.

"Really, a right hook—that's your play?" came the voice.

How did he know I was ready to punch him?

"I've got cameras everywhere, pet. Now, be a good girl and sit in the red chair."

"No," I hissed. "You aren't the boss of me. I demand you let me out of here."

At that, he chuckled. I expected him to give me another order, or to shove his way inside. If he did, I planned to tackle him with all my might—knee to the groin, then run like hell. But he didn't say anything. In fact, it was eerily quiet.

Until it wasn't. There was a knock on a door other than mine.

"Gwen, sit in the yellow chair. I'm coming in." Brooks' voice was calm, collected, and utterly terrifying.

Who was Gwen? Was that my neighbor in the vent? I walked over to the door and pressed my ear against it, trying to hear over the pounding of my heart.

"Yes, Master," came a weak reply.

The sounds of a cage being unlocked...and then screams. Lots of them. A moment later, my door rattled as though something had been thrown against it. I took a step back in horror.

"Gwen, why don't you tell our new pet, Amanda, what happens when she doesn't obey my commands?"

"One of us gets p-p-punished," she sobbed.

"That's right. You see, Amanda, I've found that beating or starving pets into submission is slow and tedious, but playing on their compassion...ah, that's where the female sex is at its weakest. For every minute you disobey me, it's one fingernail Gwen loses. Have you ever had a fingernail ripped off, Amanda? Gwen has. It's quite painful, isn't it, my pet?"

"Yes, Master." Her whimpering was that of a woman steeling herself against impending torture. It made me sick to my stomach.

"Now, I'll say this one more time, Amanda. Sit in the red chair."

Another scream from Gwen.

"All right! All right! I'll sit in your damn chair!" I shrieked.

"Move faster," he snapped.

With my heart racing, I threw my fists to my sides and went to sit in the red chair that was close to the wall of windows, several yards away from the door. Even if I ran, I'd never make it to the door before he shut himself in here with me.

"Now, stay," he ordered.

There was a shuffling outside, then a thunk and three beeps as he locked Gwen back in her room.

"Cross your ankles, dear," my captor demanded. "You look like a whore sitting like that."

With nostrils flaring at the camera monitoring me from above the door, I crossed my ankles.

"Hands on your lap where I can see them."

I complied, gritting my teeth in both anger and fear.

That's when he finally opened my cage.

CHAPTER SIX

Connor

This was how a woman should behave when a man walked into a room: silent and attentive, waiting to fulfill her master's wishes. She'd get there—of that I had no doubt. They all did, eventually. Amanda was hardly any different. She was more defiant than most, but that would make housebreaking her more of a thrill. There was something titillating about watching the fight in a person's eyes slowly fade, until the only thing left was utter compliance. Once they accepted their fate, they were fully trained. There was still a raging fire to Amanda, so she might very well take a few weeks longer than most. That was fine by me: more time to play with her before I sent her off to her new master.

"I've come to take your photo," I said, holding up the camera. The door locked into place behind me as I sat on the couch opposite her. There was no fear in her escaping. The thumbprint scanner ensured I was the only one who could open the door. There was nothing in the unit she could use against me, and I was easily twice her size. Even if she got a blow in, she wouldn't live to see a second. There was no escape. The only way out of this cage was if I allowed her to leave.

"Who are you?" she shouted. "What do you want with me?"

A slow smile spread across my lips. Always the same asinine

questions. I should make a recording so I didn't have to repeat myself time and time again, but there was a cheap thrill in watching reality set in with each new detail a pet received.

"You know my name. It's Connor Brooks. Not my legal name, obviously, but while you're in my care you can call me 'Master.'"

"Screw you," she spat.

"Oh, that will come, don't you worry. But first, I need photos." I moved over to the dining area and adjusted the legs of the tripod, while Amanda watched in fear.

"Let me go! What do you want? I don't have any money."

Placing the camera on the tripod, I scanned the room for the best light. "I told you. I want to take your picture."

She got up, then, and lunged at me. It would have been comical, if not so predictable. She didn't even land one punch before I had her on the ground, my knees caging her forearms as she squirmed beneath me. With practiced ease, I wrapped one hand around her neck and applied just enough pressure—not enough to kill her, but enough to let her know who was in charge. After she turned three shades of red, she finally stopped fighting.

"Good girl." I released my hand, but kept my knees on her arms. This was a good angle. I leaned over and grabbed the camera off the tripod, pointing the lens at Amanda's still-blotchy face. Her fiery hair sprayed wildly around her like a halo, and her eyes were glassy from the exertion, making her look positively broken. It was beautiful. I took several shots as she angled her head away from me. It only made her more appealing.

"I'm going to let you up now. When I do, you're going to go over to the dining room table and sit on it. Understood?"

She glared at me. My hand went to her throat again. "I asked you a question. Do you understand?"

Coughing against my grip, she nodded her head vigorously.

I lifted one knee off her arm, and Amanda immediately brought her hand up to massage her throat. Slowly, I took my other leg off and stood up. She lay on the floor for a few moments to catch her breath, until I kicked at her to get up.

"On the table."

She stood up, her legs slightly shaky. Her skirt had twisted itself up her thighs, but she made no effort to fix it. Before she got to the table, however, I gave her the next command.

"Lose the skirt."

Amanda froze where she stood. With her back to me, her shoulders tensed, as a quick intake of air passed her lips.

"Are you going to rape me?"

Her voice was small. It pleased me.

"Do you want me to?" I asked. She shook her head. "Some women find that wildly erotic. They even pay men to perform such a service. It's a deeply disturbing world we live in."

"No, I would not like to be raped," she said, her voice weak.

"Good, because I have no immediate plans to do so." I could sense her relief, so I continued. "However, when I *do* fuck you—and trust me, I will—it will only be *after* you have begged me to take you." She turned her head to look at me in horror. It was priceless. "Consent is so important," I added with a grin. "All of my pets give me their consent. You will too."

"I will never—"

"That's what they all say." I sighed. "And guess what? They all do." I nodded at the table. "Now, lose the skirt and hop that fine ass onto the table."

I didn't know what kind of man Malcolm was—a leg man, an ass man, tits? I had no clue what he preferred, so I'd need to cover all my bases. It was strange working with so little guidance on a potential client's kink. It made it harder to know how to position the pet. Were they into bondage, dominance, submission, role play, or a foot fetish? Ideally, the adoption photos would lean into their kink, but Malcolm was a big question mark—not that I was going to mind exploring all the options with this one. I'd had a semi for her from the second I had walked into the room. There was something about this woman that was wildly attractive to me, and I couldn't quite figure out what it was.

I wasn't lying about not being a rapist, though. I might have been a lot of things, but that wasn't one of them. Sure, I took the things in life I wanted, but sex…that was something I needed given freely to me. I wanted to possess my pets, not dominate them. There was a difference. The pets begged me to fuck them, and I gave them what they asked for. Amanda would ask for it too. Once she accepted that, her life would be much easier.

Until then, it was playtime.

AMANDA

My throat was still on fire from where he'd strangled me. The stars hadn't fully left my vision, and now he wanted me to take off my skirt as well? What sort of freak *was* this guy? There should have been some relief knowing he didn't plan to rape me, but his confidence that I'd beg to sleep with him left my whole body cold.

How many others had he done this to?

"Amanda, you're stalling. Take off the skirt. I would like to go home at some point… unless you'd like me to stay the night?" he asked.

My fingers flew to my skirt, quickly pulling down the zipper. No way in hell did I want him to stay over. Swallowing down my fear, I let the skirt fall at my feet.

"Good girl. Now, kick it over to me."

I glanced down at the dark fabric at my feet. I was mostly covered, thanks to the length of the button-down shirt I wore, but I was still very much exposed. For the moment, he held the power in the room until, I could find something I could use as a weapon, or some way out. The only play I had was to do whatever he asked of me.

I hooked the skirt on my foot and kicked it toward him. He bent down and tucked it into his back pocket. "You won't be needing that anymore. Now, plant that fanny on the table."

My legs shook as I walked to the table, but that was when I

noticed the table was also welded to the floor. Just as the table and chair had been in the bedroom.

"Ah, yes, you'll note all of the furniture is secured. Prison-grade accommodations. I spared no expense on your cage. I've also removed anything you might use as a weapon: no towels, no silverware, no toiletries. That's not to say you won't earn those privileges with time," Connor added, taking a few steps toward me. His fingers brushed a lock of my hair, and it was all I could do not to bite his hand for trying. "Your cage is empty until you earn amenities. My pets work on a reward system." The smile he wore on his face made me sick.

"Why do you keep calling me a 'pet'?"

"Because that's what you are—a stray human with no home. How sad. Lucky for you, I'm fostering you until I can find you a good forever home with a high-paying buyer. Like any good foster situation, I'll teach you proper etiquette for your new owners in the meantime. Now, let's take some adoption photos, shall we? If your training goes well, I'll have you in your new home by the end of the month."

My mouth dropped open. *He was going to sell me?* The room spun a little as I felt the color drain from my body.

"Perch that ass on the table, and lift your legs like you're at the gynecologist."

"You can't be serious," I gasped.

Before I even saw his hand move, I felt a sting of pain across my right breast. He'd slapped me. Hard.

"The next one lands on your face, and it'll be a punch, not a slap. I'm in charge. Nod to indicate to me that you understand."

Stunned, I nodded.

"Get on the table. I will not repeat myself again."

Recoiling from the evil emanating from his pores, I did as he instructed. Even at his drunkest, Sam had never pulled twisted shit like this. Still, I knew better than to anger an abuser. It only made the punishment worse. It was far better to disconnect from the situation as best you could—to turn into a robot, follow orders, and make a plan to escape another day. The only directive now was to survive.

Photo after photo, I did as he bid. I didn't bother to cry. I knew tears would do me no good. He wanted me to follow orders, so I gave him everything he wanted. The only saving grace was that he hadn't asked me to take off my blouse or my underwear.

Yet.

"Hop off the table and lean your torso over it. Tilt that ass high in the air for me."

Numb, I did as he said. At least I didn't have to look at him this way. He walked over, lifted my shirt off my backside, and I froze.

"Relax. If I wanted to fuck you, I would have already." His hand, however, lingered on my ass but I was too scared of what he'd do to me if I tried to move it.

A few shots of me spread out like that, and he was finished.

"That should do it, for now. If I get a nibble and they want more detailed shots, I'll be back. I don't post full nudes on the adoption files. You're welcome. If they want the milk, they have to pay for the cow." He winked at me, and I wanted to punch him.

As I righted myself, Connor gathered his tripod and camera, and without another word, he left me alone in the unit.

Thunk. Beep. Beep. Beep.

Shivering, I stood stock still until I heard the ding of the elevator. After pressing my ear to the door to confirm he was gone, I rushed over to the kitchen vent and peered through the wire grate.

"Gwen!" I shouted. "Are you alright?" Her screams from earlier still reverberated in my mind. She didn't answer at first, but after a moment, the mattress moved enough to see that she had sat down on her bed.

"I'm okay," she said. "He didn't take a nail this time. Thank you for complying so fast. Most don't."

"What did he do to you? How long have you been here? What the hell is going on, Gwen?"

Her foot twitched, then disappeared onto the mattress. "First of all, my name isn't Gwen—that's what my new owner has named me. The guy he's selling me to has a thing for Gwyneth Paltrow. He's making me grow my hair out to look more like her. I'm nearly as skinny as she is now, thanks to the scraps he feeds me. I imagine once I reach that weight, I'll be sold."

"What's your real name?" I asked, trying to keep the horror from my voice and failing miserably.

"Kelli. Kelli Turner."

"Hi, Kelli. I'm Amanda. I came here to look at an apartment for rent, and that jackass locked me inside."

"Let me guess, you replied to an ad for a studio apartment, great view, $650 a month?" Kelli asked.

I swallowed hard. "A one-bed for $750."

"Yeah. Guess we should've known that was too good to be true, huh?"

I felt the hairs on the back of my neck raise, absorbing all of this. "So that's his game. He lures women into these units, then locks them in?"

"Yep. As far as I can tell, there are four of us up here now, but who knows how many more he might have out of earshot—or how many have come before us."

I thought back to when we had first gotten off the elevator. There were at least ten units on this floor. Was the whole building like this? Filled with women?

"How long have you been here?" I asked.

The mattress squeaked, and her left foot reappeared. "I don't know. I used to mark the drywall with my fingernails, but he tore off a nail once he found out I was doing it. He didn't want me to have any sense of time. At that point, it had been thirty-six days. If I had to guess, I'd say three months, maybe more."

Three *months*...

"Has he taken photos of you yet?" she asked.

"He just took some. What does it mean?" I pressed myself closer to the floor, as Kelli's voice was hard to hear.

"It means he likely has a buyer lined up. You could be out of here tomorrow, next week, next year...depends on the market," she said, disgusted. "Master's job is to break your spirit and make you comply with your new owner's wishes. They'll instruct him on what kind of training they want before they're willing to adopt you. In my case, my owner wants me rail-thin and primed for anal sex. So yeah, he's 'training' me to take it." Her voice seemed so far away. Hopeless. "If you want to survive, you'll learn to listen quickly. Master doesn't like to repeat himself. And the sooner you're 'housebroken,' the sooner you'll get out of this shithole."

"And go where?" I gasped.

"To whoever buys you. It has to be better than here. It just has to."

There was something so broken in Kelli's voice. She'd accepted her reality. She'd given up. No way in hell was that ever going to be me. I'd find a weakness in Connor's system, or in him. Every man had a soft spot, especially the abusers—you simply needed to know where to look.

And I had lots of practice in that department.

CHAPTER SEVEN

Connor

Sighing, I went to my desk with a headache. I'd taken a brief nap to rid myself of it, but it hadn't helped. Work demands would be at an all-time high today, and my first thoughts went to Amanda.

Even without seeing her adoption photos, I knew they wouldn't work for Malcolm. She had pretended to be strong, but there was fear in her eyes. While that was a turn-on for many buyers, I knew it would probably make Malcolm squirm. For someone so high up in the black market, you'd think he'd be used to shady shit, but some men stayed on their high horses and didn't want to mess with human trafficking. Annoying, but understandable. The risks were a tad harsher when you gambled in my game, even though I only traded in adult pets, much to the dismay of many of my buyers. The legalities when it came to minors weren't worth the risk. Adult women were far more disposable in the eyes of the law—much easier to buy off a cop with an adult. If buyers wanted children, they'd have to go elsewhere. I might not have many lines, but that was one of them.

It was a risky job, being a pet store owner. I had to be meticulous when finding foster homes for the pets. It wasn't about selling to the highest bidder, either—it was who could be the most discreet with their ownership, who would be willing to sign the

NDA, who I could trust to keep our twisted little secret. That was paramount. One loose lip, and the whole operation would fall apart. With Malcolm, I could leverage what I knew of his business against him to ensure his silence, but I wasn't worried about that. Convincing him that he wanted to adopt was the bigger issue.

A reshoot would be inevitable, once Amanda had settled in and accepted her fate. In the meantime, I had other matters to attend to, like making sure the trash removal was completed. Then, I'd need to focus on the transfer of Gwen to her new owner next week. As if that wasn't enough, there was now the matter of finding a new pet to replace Stacey, the one I'd lost to stupidity. This job was nonstop.

After slipping into some sweatpants for the night, I made a few calls for tomorrow's deadlines. While I was on hold for Kenny, I pulled up the cameras from Stacey's apartment. The cleaning crew had arrived before my nap. They knew their instructions, and didn't need me to oversee things. The black garbage bags were gone, as was all the blood from the tub where they had chopped Stacey into small pieces to avoid carrying out a body bag. That would raise an eyebrow on the streets, but several black garbage bags? Done and done. Glancing at the clock, I noted they'd made good time.

On the third ring, Kenny answered. "I'm on my way to the firepit," he said, anticipating my call. "Firepit" was the code word we used for the crematorium. The cleaners were paid handsomely for their ask-no-questions arrangement.

"I was just admiring your work. Looks nice and clean," I said. "Any hiccups?"

"No, we're on target. We should be finished in about an hour."

"Call me when it's done."

"Yes, sir."

Hanging up, I leaned back in my chair and rubbed my eyes before I checked on the others. Gwen was on her bed, staring up at the ceiling as she often did. Belinda, my poor German girl who didn't understand a thing I said to her, was cowering in the shower, huddled up like a mouse. She'd break within a few weeks. For now, the other units sat empty. Pets came to me in waves: all at once, or not at all. I felt fortunate to have so many pending sales.

My attention drifted to Amanda's cage last. Predictably, she was searching the unit for weapons or a way out, of which there was none. She was still clinging to hope. Silly girl. She'd learn soon.

With all my fosters safely accounted for, I begrudgingly transferred ten grand into my dad's account. He didn't deserve the bailout, not after being the shit father he was, and I knew this wouldn't be the last time he called needing help. It was pathetic how he groveled. I wished I could say that this was his way of mourning my mom's death, but he'd always been weak. Gullible. I didn't know how she'd put up with him, or why she'd never punished him for his mistakes the way she had me. Maybe then he would have learned. She'd had a soft spot for him. He was her one and only weakness, something I'd never allow to happen to me.

No one was getting inside my heart. Ever.

My eyes darted to the small frame on my desk, which held a picture of my mother. Her long locks were drawn into a severe bun, pulled so taught it erased the smile lines around her eyes— not that she had ever smiled much. Dad was the only one who could get her to laugh. I envied him that. Try as I might, I had never gotten her to respond kindly to anything I did. I had wanted so much to please her.

Still, without her, none of this would have been possible.

"Connor, to your cage."

"But Mother, I did as you asked. I poured out Daddy's bourbon."

"You didn't empty the one he keeps inside the toilet."

My eyes widened. I didn't think she knew he kept one there. He'd made me promise never to tell her about that one. He'd said it was the only thing keeping him with us—that if she took away his drink, he'd leave. The balance of losing my father or displeasing my mother was an impossible task for an eight-year-old.

"I didn't know he kept one there," I lied. I could feel my limbs begin to shake.

"Connor, I didn't raise you to lie to me. Now, into your cage."

I hated that tears were forming in my eyes, but I hated the cage more. It was so cold. So lonely. "But Mother, I was just there yesterday."

"And this time, you shall be in there for longer. Without food. That will teach you not to defy me."

My stomach rumbled with the threat of her warning. In the past, she'd only made me stay in the cage for a day, but at least she had brought me food —I could make the time pass quicker if I rationed it throughout the day. What would hold my sanity if I didn't have food to keep me going?

Looking up at her stern eyes, I knew that arguing against her command would do no good, nor would yelling for my dad to help. If he'd been fighting with Mother, he would have left the house in search of more bourbon, and when he came home, he would be of little use to anyone.

Reluctantly, I hung my head and walked down to the basement. My mother followed close at my heels. She opened the metal dog crate, and I climbed inside. I noticed she'd removed the pillows that used to be there. Now it was just a metal wire box. She shut the door behind me, and put the padlock on.

"I know you don't understand this, Constantine, but this is for your own good. You must learn how to take charge in life. If you have a husband who drinks, you find a way to make that end. If you have a son who lies to you, you cage him until he sees things the proper way. I do this not to punish you, but to protect you. To ensure that you don't become soft like your father. The world is cruel—the sooner you learn that, and discover how to turn that cruelty to your benefit, the better."

Rubbing my eyes to try and erase the memory, I pushed out of my chair and made my final round of lock checks—not that anyone could escape. Still, it was a habit. As I walked, I found my eyes drifting toward Amanda's door. I walked over to her screen, let it scan my face, and scrolled until I found which room she was in, curious to see what she was up to.

AMANDA

Try as I might, I couldn't get Kelli to talk to me anymore. All she'd said was that it wasn't safe, that he'd be watching. I didn't doubt her. The cameras were everywhere. Connor wasn't subtle about their placement, didn't even *try* to hide them. They were all secured to the apartment's high ceilings, with no chance to reach them to cover their view. If I had to guess, every inch of this place was monitored. How had I missed the cameras when I first entered the unit?

Because you weren't counting on being kidnapped when you came to look for an apartment. In hindsight, it wouldn't have mattered even if I had. I was Connor's prisoner the second he shut that door. I had been a fool, and walked right into his trap.

It was all starting to make sense now, like those random questions on the rental application that had no right being there: marital status, next of kin, and employment history. He had to have used the answers to those applications to weed out the people who had loved ones that would notice if they went missing. Who did I have—my dad? It wasn't likely he'd try to find me. He'd given up on me long ago. I hadn't spoken to him in years, and didn't know where he lived, or even if he was alive.

Outside of my father, I didn't have anyone close to me. I'd come here to make a fresh start, leaving a bad job and an even worse relationship behind. I'd cut ties with everyone—and somehow, Connor knew it. I had made myself the ideal pawn for his twisted game. I'd thought I'd seen the worst of human behavior with Sam—another situation I should have run from, another man I thought I could fix. When would I learn that men like him couldn't be fixed?

Or worse, that I wasn't the type of woman men changed for?

After the tenth walk around the apartment, finding nothing of use for a weapon or escape, I curled up on the green chair, shivering against the approaching night. The place had no blankets or pillows, nothing with which to cuddle up against to feel safe. That was, no doubt, part of the plan—strip away all creature comforts, as they do in a prison, to break someone's spirit. But Connor didn't know that my spirit was already as hard as nails. I could take whatever he dished out. I was used to abusive men. I knew their games. I would find a way out of here, or die trying.

That was when I heard a strange sound. It was muffled, coming from outside my door. I tensed, waiting for Connor to barge in again, but the door stayed closed. I got up to investigate, when his voice came over the speaker.

"Sit down in the red chair."

My blood ran cold. Not wanting Kelli to pay the price for my insolence, I did as I was told.

"Place your feet on the ground, hip-width apart. Place your hands on the armrests."

I did as he commanded. For now.

"Eyes on the camera. Keep them there."

I stared at the lens waiting for him to open the door, but it never opened. Several minutes passed and he still didn't come inside. But the noise remained.

"Right there," he said. "Keep your eyes right there." There was a huskiness in his voice, one I knew well. All of a sudden, the noise made sense: he was jerking off.

Right outside my door.

"Ugnff," came his voice a moment later, followed by, "Go to sleep, pet. You're going to need your strength."

A moment later, I heard the sound of a door closing. He'd probably entered another woman's cage. I shivered.

"You okay?" It was Kelli. "How bad did he hurt you?"

Rushing over to the vent, I saw her on the floor, looking at me through the grate. Her face was pale. The hollows of her cheeks betrayed how hungry she was. Her blond hair was greasy and unbrushed. She had a small cut on her lip. How many other injuries did Kelli have?

"I'm fine. He didn't touch me, didn't even enter the apartment, but I think he jacked off in the hall. He made me sit in the chair and look at the camera, and that was it."

"Well, aren't you the special one? Normally, if he's horny, he makes us beg to be fucked by him. I don't think he's ever done that with the other girls. Consider yourself lucky. He must like you."

That was it. My way in.

I'd make Connor fall madly in love with me—then, when he wasn't expecting it, gouge his eyes out with my fingernails if I had to, bite his cock off with my teeth and make him choke on it. Then, I'd free the others.

"I'll get us out of here," I told her.

Kelli scoffed. "Sure you will. That's what we all thought, too, when we first got here." She picked herself up and flopped on her bed. "Get some sleep. It's the only real escape."

Reluctantly, I retreated to my bedroom as well. I knew falling asleep would be close to impossible, but if I was going to take Connor down, I needed all the strength I could muster. Curling myself into a tight ball, I shivered myself to sleep.

When I woke, it was to the smell of coffee and bacon—two things I knew the kitchen didn't have. I bolted up from the mattress to find Connor there, sitting across from me on the bed. There was a paper plate with scrambled eggs, two slices of bacon, watermelon, and half a slice of toast.

"Good morning, pet. Sleep well?"

Yanking my shirt down to try and cover my bare legs, I pressed myself as far away from him as I could. I hadn't even heard him come in, the curse of being a heavy sleeper.

"Not without a pillow or a blanket, I didn't," I said, rubbing a kink in my neck.

"Ah, yes, well, with time you can earn those creature comforts. I reward good behavior."

"'Good behavior?' How twisted are you?"

"Twisted? In what way am I twisted?" He was enjoying himself.

"You cage women up for fun."

He smirked at me, tenting his index fingers against his lips.

"Not for fun, Amanda, for money. There's a difference. Now, eat your breakfast before it gets cold."

I glared at the food. Even though I was starving, I didn't want to take anything he was offering. For all I knew, it was poisoned.

"I'm not hungry." My stomach growled in protest.

"Not a great liar, are you?"

"Fine. I'm hungry, but I'm not eating anything you give me."

He nodded. "You're worried it's drugged. Smart. You're right not to trust the hand that feeds you. However, I am the *only* hand that will be feeding you, and this will be the *only* meal I provide for you today. Perhaps all week. Do you want to pass that up?"

When I didn't budge, he reached out and took a large bite of my toast.

"Fine, I'll eat," I hissed. Clearly, it wasn't laced with anything.

"Good girl." A grin spread across his lips.

That was when I noticed there was no fork. "I don't have utensils."

He held up his hand and wiggled his fingers. "Ah, but you do. Ten of them."

Grinding my teeth, I reached down and took a large handful of the eggs, shoving them into my mouth as unladylike as I possibly could. That only seemed to amuse him. I chewed slowly, trying to taste if there was anything off about them. All I could make out were the eggs and the large grains of salt on top. My stomach begged for more. Feeling brave, I sampled the bacon. Perfectly crisp. I closed my eyes, and for a moment, I wasn't a prisoner: I was a little girl, sitting at my kitchen table, as my mother hummed at the stove.

The toast and fruit were up next. It was made out of some fancy bread that had lots of whole grains, and the watermelon was perfectly ripe. I hadn't eaten this well in years.

"Fattening me up for the slaughter?" I asked, taking another bite of toast.

He let out an amused burst of air. "Quite the opposite. I'm restricting your caloric intake, hence the one meal. While I appreciate your luscious curves, I suspect my buyers would prefer something a bit trimmer."

The bread stuck in my throat. He was not only holding me captive, but he was putting me on a diet. Putting my toast down, I wiped my hands against the only thing I had—my shirt.

"If you comply with my orders," he said, "I'll bring you some clothes next week."

"Next week? You expect me to walk around in this shirt until then?"

He stood up, his figure looming large over me. "Yes, I do— longer, with a mouth like that. Watch your tongue, or you'll lose what little you have on." He walked out of the bedroom and down the hall, unlocking the front door and opening it.

My body tensed. Could I make a run for it?

"Anita," he said out to the hall, "be a dear and bring me a clean towel, would you?" Connor closed the door again and leaned against it, a large Cheshire Cat grin on his face.

"Who's Anita?"

"The cleaner. You don't expect me to do it, do you?"

A glimmer of hope filled me. If there was a housekeeper, that meant there was someone out there who had free will. Someone who could call the cops. Someone who could save us.

A moment later, that someone knocked on the door. Connor deactivated the lock on the handle, and quickly took the towel.

I leaped at the chance. "Anita, help! He's keeping me against my will in here. Call the cops!"

Connor merely laughed, shutting the door. "Silly girl. Do you think she doesn't know what goes on in these rooms? She's on my payroll, and well-compensated for her work. She won't break that loyalty for you. She has a family to support and authorities to hide from, what with her undocumented status. She doesn't care about you. At the end of the day, Amanda, people are selfish. They take care of their own needs." He took the paper plate away from me. "Now, I need you to shower. You'll leave the towel at this door when you are finished with it—is that understood? If you disobey these orders, you won't get a towel again for a month."

"How am I supposed to shower without soap, or shave my legs without a razor?"

"Like I'd leave you with a razor. Silly pet." His eyes darkened, then. "Soap you earn with good behavior, and don't fret about the leg hair—it needs to grow out before it can be waxed, anyway."

"Let me guess, you have someone on payroll for that too?" I snapped, annoyed that he'd thwarted my attempt to obtain a weapon.

His eyes twinkled, almost as though he were amused by my comments. Did he not see himself as the villain in this scenario? "I have staff for everything, Amanda, but the grooming of pets I do myself. I find the experience to be quite sensual. The hot wax, the cries of pain..."

His eyes narrowed as I curled into myself a little more. This man wanted me to know he was dangerous.

"Shower. Put the towel by this door," Connor said, pointing to the exit. "I'll know if you don't follow orders." He made a small circle in the air to note his eyes in the sky.

Then, he locked me back in the cage.

CHAPTER EIGHT

Connor

Christ, that woman had spunk. I was so used to pets being submissive and cowering when I entered a room, but Amanda, while still frightened, was holding her own. That might have been the longest conversation I'd ever had with one of them. Most cried in a corner. So far, not a single tear had escaped this one.

Amanda was tough. Like me.

As much as I would've liked to have spent the rest of the day properly training her, I had too many other fires to put out—including the buyer of one currently-dead pet.

Back downstairs in my office, I called the buyer on one of my burner phones.

"Mr. Pierce, do you have a moment to talk about your foster? There's been a slight complication."

The phone on the other end shifted. "Um, give me a moment. Excuse me, Gertie, It's work. I need to take this call in the den." More shuffling and then the sound of a door closing. "I'm at home, Brooks. I told you never to call here."

"I know, and I apologize, but I have an urgent matter regarding your adoption that couldn't wait."

"What is it?"

"Well, it seems your pet is deceased."

"*What?*" he whispered. "How did that happen?"

The fewer details he knew, the better. "That's not important. What is important, however, is that I have a replacement." I clicked on a file with a new rental application: similar look to Stacey, a few inches shorter, a little lighter. Orphan. Could she be more perfect? Running a finger over the laptop image, I smirked. "She might need another week to housebreak but if you'd rather take that responsibility on yourself, it does bond a pet to their owner. Of course, I'll discount your purchase for the inconvenience."

"Yes, well, I should think so." I could hear the indecision, yes, but also the rush and thrill of breaking a pet.

"So shall I housebreak her, or would you prefer that honor? There is no greater bond than a pet to its master after it has been properly housebroken. I can tell you that from experience. I've housebroken many pets as a foster, Mr. Pierce, and even now, all these years later, if I come across one of them, you can be guaranteed that they will heel to my command—*whatever* I command."

I could almost hear him salivate at the thought of having that much control over a pet. Pierce was silent for several beats, as he no doubt weighed his options.

"What's her name?"

I smiled. She was as good as sold.

"Belinda. A very submissive German Shepard. Gorgeous coat. Great breeding hips." It was wildly amusing to make these animal innuendos, on the off-chance our conversations were being recorded. "Not a biter, unless you train her to be."

"I see." His voice was shaky, which meant he'd been turned on.

"How about I send over her adoption photos later this week," I asked, "and you can decide then?"

I hung up without letting him answer. I knew he'd text the moment he saw Belinda. She was hotter than Stacey, with bigger tits. The fact that she didn't speak the language would be the cherry on top.

With one fire out, it was time to check on the other issues. Several hours later, my deep clean was all but finished. Amanda was settling in, which meant the only one left to check on was Kelli. I'd hit her pretty hard yesterday. I might have even broken her nose, which wouldn't do at all. Sighing, I shoved out of my seat to check in on her. I'd worked too hard to model her after my client's desires, and it would suck if I'd have to set her sale date back to heal a broken face.

I lost myself to work, sorting through applications for prospective pets. The day slipped away until my stomach notified me of the time. Contemplating dinner, my office line rang. Glancing at the clock, it was likely a buyer. They tended to make contact after normal business hours, and only my dad and buyers had my office line. I wondered, briefly, if there had been an issue with the transfer, or if it was possible, that my father needed money again.

"Brooks speaking," I answered.

"Luxx here." I perked up. Malcolm Luxx never made first contact. I was always the one hounding him.

"Yes, Malcolm, what can I do for you? Finally interested in adoption?"

"Actually, that's what I'm calling about."

Well, well, well. "You're talking to the right guy. I think I've found you the perfect pet this time, an absolutely gorgeous—"

"Let me stop you there, Brooks. I'm only calling to let you know, again, that I'm not interested in *adopting* pets. I prefer to find my own...companions, thank you very much. I'm calling to ask that you please stop sending packets to my office. I don't read them, and they're problematic to dispose of."

"Mr. Luxx, you don't understand, this newest rescue—"

"Good evening, Mr. Brooks."

The bastard hung up on me, and I cursed.

No. This couldn't be the end. I knew Amanda would be perfect for him, and I just needed to figure out a way to get him to see her. Photos weren't going to cut it. He'd need to see her in the flesh, and since I knew he'd never step foot in my kennel, I'd have to bring her to him—which meant Amanda would have to be heel-trained. This was a task I usually assigned to the masters, but she would have to be an exception.

But first, I needed to check on Kelli.

AMANDA

The shower had been about as miserable as I had envisioned. With no shampoo, no soap, no shower curtain, and no bathroom door, I'd stripped off the only clothes I had, knowing full well that Connor was likely watching my naked body. I did my best to obscure the camera's view, but it was nearly impossible.

When I finished the lukewarm shower, I grabbed the towel he'd left for me, if you could even call it that. It was thin and small, more like a bathmat than a towel, and it did little to absorb much of anything. I flipped my underwear inside out and pulled them back on. The fabric stuck to my leg several times as I navigated them into place. I didn't bother to put my bra back on, since night was falling and I had so few comforts as it was. I tucked my emergency fund inside the cup and folded the bra in half. If I ever escaped from here, I would need cash to hail a cab—or buy a shotgun. Either way, the bills were a sign of hope. Once I got out, I'd have options. Not many, but better than what I had now.

Pulling on the blouse, I frowned as it gave me grief trying to slide over my damp skin. Large wet patches spread across the shirt. I was tempted to keep the towel to use as a blanket tonight, but Connor's orders had been clear. As much as I wanted to defy him, I also was in no hurry to feel his hand around my neck again.

As I was putting the towel down by the door, I heard the elevator ding.

"Shit," I whispered. I gritted my teeth, but went to sit in the chair. I crossed my ankles and placed my hands on the armrests. Better to let him think I was compliant than calculating. I'd find a fault in his systems faster if he didn't think I was a threat.

To my surprise, however, he didn't approach my door.

"Gwen, sit."

With my heart hammering, I listened as her lock came free.

"Good evening, Master," Kelli said. The door shut and locked.

Instantly, I was out of my chair. I ran over to the kitchen and pressed myself down on the floor to listen to their conversation.

"How is your face?" Connor asked. I saw the tips of his polished black shoes through the grate. Kelli's bare feet were out of sight. I couldn't see the chair she was in, but judging by her voice, it was in a corner.

"It's fine, thank you."

He walked over to her, his shadow looming large on the carpet. "Hmm. Doesn't appear broken. A bit of a black eye, but that can be covered."

"Yes, Master."

"For being such a good pet," he said, "I thought I'd offer you a reward. What would please you?"

Kelli was quiet for a moment. I wanted to scream at her to tell him to go to hell, but instead, she whispered something low that I couldn't make out.

"What's that, pet? I couldn't hear you. Speak up."

Kelli cleared her throat. "I would like you to fuck me, Master."

He let out a pleased laugh. "Beg me."

My blood ran cold. It was as he'd predicted: Kelli was literally about to *beg* her kidnapper to have sex with her. My stomach lurched.

"Please, Master, I beg you. Please, fuck me."

"Stand up."

The chair creaked as she followed his orders.

"Take your shirt off. Stand against that wall."

I heard the light sound of falling fabric, before her bare feet stepped directly in front of the grate.

No. He wasn't about to screw her where I could see?

I started to push myself up off the floor when I heard my name.

"Stay right where you are, Amanda—I know you're watching us," Connor said. "It's time you get a glimpse into your future."

Frozen, I hovered where I was. How could he know I was here? He wasn't in the hall looking at my screen. He was bluffing.

"I have your cameras on my phone, pet," he sneered. "I can see your wet hair dripping dangerously on that white blouse. No bra, too. How delightful."

Fuck.

"Now, plant your ass back down and pay attention. This'll be you very soon."

I didn't budge for a moment. Then, Kelli screamed.

"I won't ask again," he hissed.

Not seeing much of a choice, I lowered myself down and looked through the grate once again. Kelli's heels were pressed against it. His black shoes came closer to her.

"Such good girls I've raised," he purred. "Gwen, take my pants off. With your teeth."

"Yes, Master."

My nostrils flared. No way would I do that. I'd bite his dick off if he ever let me that close to it, a defense I'd keep close to the vest. It might be my only ticket out of here.

A moment later, his pants pooled at his ankles.

"That's it," Connor whispered. "Now, turn around."

Kelli's feet spun around to face me.

"Spread your legs."

Her feet moved out of view, but his remained center stage.

There was a slight cry from Kelli as I felt the wall vibrate. Then, the sound of flesh smacking rhythmically against flesh. The moment of full penetration was normally a turn-on during sex, but I couldn't help but feel sick to my stomach.

"My God, Gwen, you are so wet. Have you been thinking about me all day?"

"Yes, Master," she moaned. If I didn't know better, it would have sounded like she was enjoying herself.

The walls shook more before Connor suddenly stopped, ordering her to get on the floor. He'd positioned her ass right where I could see it. The fucker wanted me to watch. Pinching my eyes shut, I swallowed the bile.

"Now, now, Amanda. How will you ever learn how I like to fuck with your eyes closed?"

My eyes flicked open, and I saw his face looking back at me through the grate. I gasped and shoved away.

"Eyes on the prize, Amanda. Or do I need to break Gwen's nose for real this time?"

Kelli whimpered, and I knew I couldn't do that to her. Disgusted, I moved back to the grate and stared the beast down.

"Good girl. I won't warn you again. Disobey me, and your friend here pays the price. If you step a toe out of line, Amanda, I will punish each and every girl here, and I will make them know you're to blame. Do you understand?" He smacked Kelli's ass, hard. Brutally. She held in a whimper. "Answer me, Amanda."

"Alright! Alright! I understand!" I screeched.

"Tsk-tsk-tsk. That's not how we talk to our owners, is it, Gwen? What should she have said, pet?"

"Yes, Master," Kelli parroted.

"That is correct. Well done. Now, you try it, Amanda."

My nostrils flared. He was such an asshole. Kelli's muffled cry sounded in my ears.

"Yes, Master," I seethed.

"What was that? I didn't quite catch that."

"Yes, Master!" I shouted.

"There, was that so hard?" Connor lowered himself over Kelli. Impossibly strong thighs and a tight ass became visible through the grate. He brought his hand down around his long length, positioning himself to enter her.

"Are you ready for me to come inside you?" he asked.

"Yes, Master. Please," Kelli whimpered.

"Amanda, are you ready?"

I clenched my teeth. "Yes, Master."

In the blink of an eye, his shaft disappeared into her folds, showing how horrific this nightmare I was trapped in was about to become.

CHAPTER NINE

Connor

Once I'd removed the condom and cleaned myself up, I left Gwen sitting in her chair. She'd obeyed well, and was ready for her new foster home. As tempted as I was to visit Amanda after such a successful first lesson, I knew that she needed to sit with her fears about what I would do to her next. That's where so many traffickers went wrong: they didn't allow enough time for the brainwashing to set in. Fear was a motivator, sure, and it could produce moderate compliance, but for the type of product I was pushing, you needed absolute control, and you couldn't get that with fear alone. You needed to create loyalty. Utter and complete devotion. It started as fear, then desperation, bargaining, and pleading, but eventually it all turned into hopelessness. That's when a person became truly compliant, when the women finally accepted their place. If you moved them into their new home before that stage, you'd have a dangerous pet on your hands.

Once I was back in my apartment and had put the security systems in place, I yanked off my jacket, undid my shirt, and kicked off my shoes. A hot shower was calling my name. While I always used a condom with pets, I still showered off their scent after. If I was honest, they disgusted me—not just the hygiene restrictions that I placed upon them, but the fact that I was using someone else's toy. They would never be as compliant with me as they would be with their owners, which was how it should be. I'd long debated getting a pet of my own to tend to my sexual satisfaction, but there had never been any I felt I wouldn't tire of after a few months. I did envy the owners that—someone always being there to fulfill their desires. Not that I couldn't bend the fosters to my will, mind you, but it didn't seem to be the same as some of the relationships I'd arranged in recent years. Some of the pets seemed truly happy with their owners...whatever that meant.

Absently, I wondered if Amanda could be someone I saw as my own pet. She was a spitfire. Once she was broken, she would be the ultimate trophy. Surely, I didn't want to give that prize away?

I shook my head. "No, Connor. You got her for Malcolm. Pull your shit together." Unzipping my pants, I went into the shower to wash away all thoughts of Amanda.

When I awoke in the morning, it was with a jolt. "The towel."

I had completely forgotten to get the towel back from Amanda. On the surface, nothing to worry about, but fresh on the heels of Stacey's recent suicide, I found myself wondering if Amanda could have reached such levels of desperation so soon. Doubtful, but not impossible. A person could easily tear that thin towel into strips, tie them together, and...

I flung the sheets off my bed, still naked from the night before, and bolted to the screening room. Pulling up her unit, I scanned the living room. The angle of the camera made it impossible to see if the towel was there. There was a spot of about two feet by the foot of the door that I couldn't see, a problem I'd have to remedy. Amanda wasn't in the living room. My eyes darted to the kitchen, then the bedroom. Still, nothing. She wasn't in the bathroom, either.

Cursing, I ripped open my door and marched down the hall, waiting impatiently for the facial scan to complete.

Thunk. Beep. Beep. Beep.

I turned the handle and stepped inside, expecting to see a dead body hanging from one of the light fixtures. There was nothing out of the ordinary. Shutting the door behind me, I nearly tripped on something. The towel. Bending down, I picked it up. It was slightly damp from her shower.

Where was she?

Narrowing my eyes, I tiptoed toward the bedroom. If Amanda was trying to jump me, she would have the surprise of her life. Twisting the towel in my hands, I pulled it tight between my fists. I wouldn't hesitate to choke the life out of her if she tried anything.

Entering the bedroom, I scanned the space. She wasn't on the mattress, and there was no one hiding in the corners. The closet was empty. I inched my way into the bathroom, prepared for a jump scare, but she wasn't there either.

That's when I heard a soft snore. Whipping my head around, I found her—curled into a tight ball on the floor between the mattress and the wall. The mattress had hidden her from my initial view.

Relief flooded over me—not just for a lost pet, but because *she* hadn't left me.

Connor, don't fall for a pet.

Ignoring my thoughts, I gently climbed onto the mattress and laid down beside her. Amanda's face was to me, her back pressed against the wall, but she seemed at peace. Calm. Her thin white shirt did little to cover her, with her whole ass hanging out in favor of her neck being warm.

I wasn't sure why, but I found myself draping the towel over her body. She let out a delighted sigh as she accepted the newfound warmth. A slight smile danced across her lips, and I felt my heart rate accelerate. She was stunning.

Logic told me I should go back to my unit, knowing that the product was safe, but I didn't want to leave. Instead, I tucked my arm under my head and watched her sleep, until I drifted off myself.

AMANDA

When I awoke, I nearly screamed—not because I realized I hadn't been dreaming and I *was* being held captive—but because Connor was on my bed.

Very, very naked.

He was lying on his back, sprawled out and vulnerable like a starfish. He seemed to be asleep. I was still on the floor, so I sat up as quietly as I could, only to notice the forbidden towel had been placed on top of me.

How long had he been here?

Clutching the towel to my chest, my eyes darted back down to Connor. It was impossible not to look at him. Despite being a twisted fuck, the man was undeniably beautiful—built to the point of Greek god status, with a jawline that could cut marble. Even flaccid, he was massive.

I looked down again at the towel in my hands. Could I use this as some sort of weapon, cover his mouth with it and strangle him? I shook the thought away. He'd quickly overpower me.

Come on, Amanda. What could you do to take advantage of this situation? He's in your bed, naked. Even if I bit his dick off right here and now, how would I get out of the apartment? I needed his fingerprint, and he wasn't about to willingly let me go after that. If I touched him now, it would mean my death.

Unless...

Whenever Sam had come home dangerously drunk, two things would go down: either he'd beat me senseless, being careful not to hit my face where it would be visible to others, or he'd want to fuck. I got good at choosing the lesser of two evils. The second he'd come home, eyes glossed over, I'd turn on the seductive charms—get him to exert the last of his energy inside me, then pass out from exhaustion. If I could do the same with Connor, it might endear him to me. Maybe he'd let something slip, give me something as a reward for good behavior that I could turn around and use on him. It was worth a shot.

Connor was smart, though, not a hulking idiot like Sam. I'd have to be convincing.

CONNOR

I woke to the feeling of warmth and wetness against my chest, and my body kicked into reaction mode. In an instant, I had whoever was on top of me on their back in a chokehold. Beneath me, Amanda gasped for air. I let her go, trying to assess what had happened. She reached up to rub her neck as she sat up in the bed. She'd been lying beside me. *She* had been the warmth.

"What do you think you're doing?" I hissed.

"You looked cold," she said. "I was trying to warm you up."

"What?"

Her eyes fell to the ground. "I was cuddling you."

I raised an eyebrow. Looking down at my pec, I noticed a shimmer of wetness there. "With your lips?"

She looked up at me and bit her bottom lip seductively. My dick twitched.

"Was that wrong of me to do?"

My heart did that weird racing thing again, but I shoved the feeling down. "Yes, that was wrong. You don't get to touch me unless I command it." I stood up from the mattress to face her, still very much naked and trying very hard to keep an erection at bay. The wounded look in her eyes hurt. Odd. I'd never given a rat's ass about a pet's feelings before. Why should it matter now?

"As punishment," I said, "I'm going to need your shirt." I held my hand out.

Her eyes widened, but then she swallowed. She unbuttoned the shirt and slipped out of it, so that she was standing in just her panties.

Cue the erection.

Damn it. I couldn't let her see that she had that power over me.

I quickly bent down and grabbed the towel from her, as well as the bra she had folded neatly beside the bed. As I lifted it, a roll of bills fell to the floor. Her rent money. I retrieved it, clutching the money in my hand, and marched out of the room before my body could betray what I'd wanted to do to her.

Locking her back up in her cage, I leaned my head against the door, fighting every urge I had to go back in there and take her. I could, too—easily—and had, several times over, with the other pets. The only difference was that *I* was the one taking them. If I went back in there, it would be Amanda taking over me, and that was something I couldn't allow. Ever.

CHAPTER TEN

Amanda

He took my money. My *hope*.

I wanted to cry, to scream at the top of my lungs, to claw out his eyes, but mostly I was angry at myself. My plan wasn't working —or *was* it? Connor had come into my room, naked, and slept beside me, unarmed. Then...I'd gotten him aroused.

Was that why he had left so quickly—did he not want me to see that he was attracted to me? If I kept up the ruse, would he let his guard down with me? It was a slim possibility, but my only card to play.

Sitting up on the bed, I listened intently for the sound of his feet walking down the hall. After several minutes had passed, I tiptoed out to the door and pressed my ear against it, but I couldn't make out anything. The thick carpets must have muffled the sound of his departure.

I let out a breath. I'd survived another encounter with the beast. Kelli had not been so lucky last night.

Kelli. I needed to check in on her.

Walking over to the kitchen, I lay down on the ground again. The tile felt cool against my stomach without a shirt, a mild discomfort compared to that of the woman in the cage beside me.

"Kelli? Are you okay?"

There was a small sniff, but other than that, she didn't answer.

"Kelli, please talk to me. I'm worried about you. Did he hurt you?"

At that, she laughed. "And what are you going to do about it if he did? Please, enlighten me, newbie. How are you going to avenge me, sitting in a cage as secure as mine?"

"I don't know," I confessed. "Yet."

"I'm fine," Kelli said eventually. "He never hurts his pets enough to leave permanent damage. We're worth money to him."

"Right," I said. "So I have to wait him out, wait until he gives me something I can use against him. Like maybe a pencil? Hell, even a fork could work."

Kelli scoffed. "He's not going to give you shit. Oh, he'll tell you he will, if you're good—if you've earned it—but he won't. He'll never give you a creature comfort, not so much as a towel to dry off from the shower. You have to shiver and air-dry, huddled in a corner like an animal."

"He gave me a towel," I said.

"He did?"

"Um, yeah. Yesterday. I mean, I didn't get to keep it, but he let me use it to dry off."

A low whistle came through the grate. "Guess you're something special, then—or he's getting soft. What I wouldn't give for a real shower, cozy pajamas, and a hot cup of tea." I heard her murmur to herself at the fantasy. "I can only hope my next master will be kinder."

I pushed myself up to sit, wanting to know more. "When you're sold, you'll find a way to escape your new location. It's got to be less advanced than this shit."

"Escape? I'm not planning to escape," Kelli scoffed.

"What?"

Kelli let out a small laugh. "I remember when I was as naïve as you. When I thought Master would slip up, make a mistake. Give me an out he hadn't planned on. Wake *up*, girl. He's been doing this for years by the sounds of it. He knows what he's doing.

According to Connor, if we run from our new owners, his thugs will hunt us down, and our new masters will decide if we live or die. What our punishment will be for disobeying is up to them. You need to wake up, Amanda. You're no longer a free woman. You're Connor's property. Even after he sells you, he ensures you remain compliant. If not, you or someone you care about is taken out."

"Well, he'll be hard-pressed to find someone he can hold over me. I don't have a family to hurt," I said, but even as I said it, my thoughts drifted to my absent father, then to Rita, whose couch I'd crashed on before coming here, then to the people I'd worked with in Seattle. While they weren't exactly close, I didn't want to see them hurt on my account. I had no doubts Connor would know information about every single one of them too.

"We're done here," Kelli said. "I've paid enough for your rebellion lately."

A wave of guilt washed over me. She was right—that was twice now she'd been punished for something I'd done. I had to be smarter. If not for my sake, then for hers.

CONNOR

After leaving Amanda with a hard-on, I jacked off and took a cold shower. I was horny, that was all. It had nothing to do with her. Thinking clearly again, I went over to my safe and dug out an ankle monitor. I had to get Amanda sold off, and fast, before she messed with my mind any further. I couldn't afford to be as reckless as I had been this morning. These were pets, not lovers.

Amanda had been the only pet to have ever cock-teased me like this, which meant she was a liability. I needed to get rid of her fast. I wouldn't be able to train this one, not if I was going to get hard every time I was in the same room with her, and that meant I needed her sold off. Like, yesterday.

Since Malcolm wouldn't take my deliveries, I'd have to bring her to him. Once he saw Amanda in the flesh, he wouldn't be able to resist her.

A plan formulated in my head. Picking up my phone, I dialed Patricia. She wasn't due in until Monday, but she'd get the message and have what I needed by the time I got out of bed. She was efficient that way.

"Patricia, I need an invite for two to Malcolm's. I know he always does something for his birthday." I scrolled through my calendar. "It's on the fifteenth."

I hung up. That was all the information she'd require. I had eight days to heel-train a pet, impossible even under the best circumstances—hence the ankle monitor. I'd do the best I could to make her obey, but I needed to ensure a safety measure should she try anything stupid.

Going to my desk, I powered up my laptop and pulled up Amanda's file. At thirty-one, she was my oldest pet to date, ancient by most clients' standards. My job was to match the owner to their perfect pet. Over the years, Malcolm had never been seen with a woman significantly younger than him—not that he'd often been seen in the company of anyone—but those rare sightings had paired him with a petite redhead at one art gallery opening, and a buxom blonde at a charity event. That was the extent of his preferences. Both times, the women were at, or near, his age.

Not a lot to go on.

Amanda ticked off the red hair and the boobs, and I held out hope that she'd be the one-two knockout Malcom was searching for. Once he saw Amanda in the dress I'd picked out for her, he wouldn't be able to resist—if he was straight, anyway. If he snubbed his nose at her, then at least I'd know to pick a different road.

If Malcom didn't take the bait, I knew that selling Amanda wouldn't be terribly hard, even at her advanced age. What she lacked in youth would be compensated for by tits and ass. In the end, men were pigs.

Scrolling over the rest of Amanda's details, I skimmed through her work history. Waitress in New York in her twenties, probably an actress with looks like hers, but there were no records of her on *IMDb*. She had stayed there a few years, then moved to Seattle, where she'd worked predominantly as a waitress in a few different bars. At some point, she had met and moved in with her abuser, Sam.

She had one living parent and no siblings. After some digging, I learned that her father lived in Florida and had remarried a woman named Flora, with whom he ran a little antique shop. Amanda was a Scorpio, which explained her feisty nature, and, judging by her first reaction to the windows, was scared of heights.

Pushing out of my chair, I went to retrieve my camera. Sliding out the data card, I placed it inside the converter and plugged it into my USB port. While the images uploaded, I went into the kitchen to make breakfast for the pets. It was an annoyance to be sure, which is why most of them got the bare minimum—just enough to keep them going until Anita could come in and provide the proper dietary restrictions needed for each pet. Some needed to lose weight, others needed to gain. People had no idea how much work went into this operation. It was exhausting.

Yanking open my refrigerator, I pulled out the eggs from yesterday, some shredded cheese, green peppers, an onion, and some sliced ham. I'd make omelets in cupcake tins—thanks, food blogs, for teaching me quick and easy ways to feed large families. This would provide enough protein to get them through until lunch.

Whisking the ingredients together, I found myself humming. I never hummed. Frowning, I poured the yolk mixture into the baking cups, topped them with cheese, then set them in the oven to bake and went back to work.

Amanda's photos, while sexy, showed a lack of emotion behind her eyes. She had clocked out. That wouldn't sell her to anyone. Zooming in, I noticed the color of her irises: so blue they were nearly black. At first, I thought it was a trick of the light, but each shot of her sported that same deep navy blue, making it hard to see where her pupils ended and the shade began. I focused my attention, next, on her lips. Her natural color peeked through the cheap lipstick she'd worn, and her shower yesterday had washed away what pigment remained, leaving her with a natural maroon. I'd read once that lip color corresponded to the shade of the nipple. My dick twitched.

"No. Jesus, Connor, she's a *pet*."

Just then, my phone dinged. It was Patricia.

"Good girl." I smiled before even reading the message. The smile instantly disappeared.

Invites secured, except it's for tomorrow at 2:00 pm, not the fifteenth. Address sent to your inbox.

"Fuck." The party was *tomorrow*? Why the hell was he having it a full week early? That wasn't enough time.

Closing the laptop, I went back to breakfast prep. Usually, I would spend time with each pet when dropping off food— checking the perimeter, training as needed—but I didn't have the time to waste. I would need to throw them the food, then spend what little time I had with Amanda getting her ready to be out in public. She would not fuck up the sale for me.

CHAPTER ELEVEN

Amanda

I was trying to brush my teeth with only my finger and the running tap when I heard a ruckus out in the hall. Heart racing, I turned off the water and ran over to the door to try and hear what was going on. At first, it was too muffled to make out, but then I heard a voice I didn't recognize.

"*Bitte, tut mir nicht!*" She sounded young, with a thick German accent. I had no idea what she was saying, but she sounded terrified.

"Take your hands off me, Belinda. Never touch a master without permission, you know that. No breakfast for you."

Thunk. Beep. Beep. Beep.

As horrific as that was to hear, I had learned a valuable lesson: don't touch Connor. He starved you when you didn't obey the rules —and because physical pain wasn't enough, he would also withhold basic human needs. Not that I should've been surprised. Why wouldn't he also take away food?

Because his pets are too valuable.

Kelli's wisdom echoed in my mind, and I clung to that thread of hope. He wouldn't let us die... he couldn't sell us if we were dead. Connor wouldn't be stupid enough to withhold food long enough to do any real damage. That knowledge was power, whether he knew it or not.

"Sit in your chair, Gwen. I'm dropping off your breakfast," Connor said. "Sorry to say, we can't play today."

Relief flooded me when I heard his voice next door. He was just the delivery boy today. *Good.* I wasn't mentally ready to deal with him again. I was still trying to process what had happened this morning. I still didn't know why he had been there when I woke, or for how long. The only thing I knew for sure was that he'd been turned on by me. He'd tried to hide his erection, but with a cock as big as his, it wasn't something easily covered. What was clear, however, was that Connor hadn't *meant* to be turned on.

This might be my way in.

My stomach rumbled with the promise of food, so preemptively, I took my spot in the wingback chair. I crossed my ankles, placed my hands on the armrests, and plastered a smile on my face. The quicker he was gone, the better.

"Well, well, well. Look who's already learned how to wait for her master," Connor cooed through the intercom. I knew he could see me through the screen. As much as I wanted to give him the finger, I didn't want to endure his rage or miss out on breakfast. So instead, I smiled brightly at him, as genuinely as I could muster.

The lock slid open, and a moment later he was inside the cage with me. The door locked swiftly behind him. In his hand, he held a small Ziplock with what looked like two corn muffins in it, and something black in his hand that I couldn't make out.

"Good morning, Amanda. I hope you're hungry?"

"I am, thank you," I said, knowing how to placate an abuser. Sam had taught me well. I would use those lessons against this asshole.

"Omelet muffins, a delicacy here. Enough protein in there to last you through lunch." He handed the bag to me.

"Thank you." I unzipped the bag and took out a "muffin." It was still warm, which meant he had either made them himself, or had them delivered. I took a bite, and my mouth watered. It was much better than I'd anticipated, full of flavor, and I let out an appreciative moan.

"I'm glad you enjoy them," Connor said. "I made them fresh for you. Maybe your next master will be kind enough to make them for you as well."

I swallowed the egg, feeling it hit my stomach like a rock. "Maybe you can show me how to make them one day?" I kept my eyes on the floor, so he wouldn't notice my attempt to endear myself to him.

"That will never happen, Amanda. In no universe am I cozying up to you in my kitchen, teaching you how to cook," he snapped. "This isn't some romance novel where the bully falls for the down-on-her-luck girl, where the power of love can change his dark ways into good." Connor walked over to me, yanking my chin up with his hand. I froze against his touch. "The sooner you come to terms with that, the better."

"Yes, Master," I forced out. I'd blown it, played my hand too soon.

"Good girl," he purred, letting me go. "I'll be spending the day with you today. I have a potential buyer for you. Normally, I wouldn't show off a foster so quickly, but this buyer seems eager for someone with your assets." He smirked, looking down at my chest.

My stomach sank. If Connor was selling me off this fast, there was no way to get into his head—but it also might mean that there could be a window of escape when he transferred me. A small sliver of hope danced in my mind.

"I can see you have questions, Amanda. You may ask them."

Since I couldn't ask the ones in my head, I decided to ask a safer one instead. "So...when I'm sold," I began, my voice strained, "what happens if they decide they don't want me?"

He sat down across from me, seemingly pleased with my question.

"We have a seven-day return policy. If a master is dissatisfied with their pet for any reason, they are returned to me, promptly punished for their actions, retrained, and resold."

"I'm never going to be free again, am I?" I asked, looking straight at him.

"No, pet. The life you knew is gone."

At least he was honest. I felt myself nod slowly. "It's okay," I sighed, "it wasn't much of a life, anyway. Can't be any worse than what I've dealt with already."

"Tell me about it—I'm genuinely curious. What was your childhood like?" Connor asked, settling into the couch.

I picked at my muffin, and decided to let him see the real Amanda. If he saw me as a human being, and not just a way to make him some money, then maybe, just maybe, there was hope.

CONNOR

As Amanda sat across from me, naked in just her panties, her breakfast barely touched, I found my eyes dancing over her skin, despite my brain telling me to look away. The bridge of her nose and the tops of her shoulders were sprinkled with freckles, the curse of a natural redhead. We didn't get a lot with her coloring, as clients preferred their pets to look more like Sleeping Beauty than Annie. I, myself, tended to be drawn to rail-thin brunettes—so why was this curvaceous, fiery beauty so appealing to me? It was difficult to keep my eyes on the movement of her full lips. I found myself wondering what they might feel like around my cock.

"Well," she began, shifting a bit, "I don't know much about my mother, other than that she died when I was little. I don't even know what of. My dad didn't know how to be a single parent. We were poor, traveled around a lot for his work. He did construction, but he couldn't afford childcare, so he'd lock me in whatever trash apartment we'd rented while he went to work. We went on like that all the way through middle school. But then, somehow, the state found out—a nosy neighbor, or something—and they took me away from him, said he was endangering me. He didn't fight it. He thought they were right, that I'd be safer in the system. I wasn't. Not by a long shot." She looked around the apartment. "So in a way, I'm used to this. Used to living in a hell I can't escape."

While I knew all of this from her file, there was something oddly familiar about her story.

"My mother used to do the same to me as a child—lock me away for days at a time." I didn't mention being placed in a dog kennel. That wasn't anyone's business.

Amanda looked at me with her big doe eyes. "Why?" She sounded genuinely horrified.

"Because I'd disappointed her. I excelled at that." Shaking my head, I refocused my attention on Amanda. I'd already told her too much. "Finish your breakfast."

She gave me a small nod, but did as she was told. When she was finished, she handed me back the bag before I had to ask for it. I slipped it into my pocket and stood up. Amanda's skin was covered in gooseflesh. Her nipples pebbled.

Damn, she was gorgeous.

"You look cold," I said, suddenly. "Here, take my shirt."

Reaching behind my neck, I grabbed the cotton fabric of my t-shirt and pulled it over my head with one fluid motion. Amanda's eyes lit up as she took in my naked torso, gaze raking over my chest and working its way down before she blushed and looked away. Pleased, I reached over and handed her my shirt. She took it and quickly pulled it over her body, blocking her best assets from me. *Good*—I needed to stay focused. But damn it all, if she didn't look even more delicious in my shirt. It swam on her, making her seem tiny and helpless.

"Thank you," she said, finally looking up to meet my eyes.

"You see? This doesn't need to be a miserable experience. A master's job is ultimately to care for their pet, in exchange for their pet's unconditional love. The sooner you give yourself over to your master, the sooner you'll have all of your needs met: mentally, physically, and most importantly, sexually."

Her eyes grew wide.

"Oh yes, Amanda," I continued, "being a pet is mostly about the sexual pleasure of the owner, but depending on the master, it can grow to be so much more. Many masters end up legally marrying their pets. It doesn't have to be miserable. The outcome is all based upon you, and how well you treat your master."

"Will you teach me?" she asked. "Will you teach me how to be a good pet?"

I felt myself smile. "I will. The first rule is to remember your role: to be at the call of your master. You must anticipate what they want, and give it to them before they even ask for it."

Amanda nodded slowly, as though understanding. "So if I were to notice that my master's eyes held sexual desire in them, I should be ready to get on my knees and pleasure them?"

My cock twitched at her words. "Correct."

At that, she slid out of her chair and crawled across the carpet to kneel in front of me. My mouth watered at the sight. Her big blue eyes looked up at me, thick with longing.

"Like this?" she asked.

No. It was against protocol to let a pet this close before they were properly trained, especially that close to your cock. One wrong bite could result in a whole slew of problems. A blow job was one luxury a foster master couldn't afford right away. A pet had to earn the right to perform one. It was far too dangerous to allow cock play in the first few weeks.

So why did I nod my permission to Amanda, allowing her to put her lips on me?

CHAPTER TWELVE

Connor

I searched Amanda's eyes for any hint of malice or deceit, but all I saw in them was lust. It made my mouth water. My cock hardened with anticipation as I allowed her hands to trace up the insides of my legs. They moved slowly, confidently. Again, I searched her eyes for trickery. Surely, this was a plan to get me off-balance. Yet the only thing I could see there was desire. For *me*. I had forgotten what it was like to be the one desired—like I was the prize, and not the vessel for punishment. I tried to think back to the last woman who had wanted me in this way, but I was finding it hard to concentrate the higher up my legs her hands went.

When her fingers landed at the top of my pants, I saw Amanda's eyes flick down, taking in the tented fabric mere inches from her hands. My hips inadvertently rocked upward, suddenly desperate for her to touch me.

"May I take you out, Master?" she purred. Another nod. I couldn't seem to find my voice. This was dangerous, reckless, and I didn't care. I wanted it. I wanted to feel her hands on me, her lips surrounding me. I needed it in a way I couldn't communicate.

With confident fingers, she slid down the elastic band of my sweatpants with ease. I lifted my hips off the chair so that she could pull the fabric down. My bare ass slapped quietly against the leather sofa. I sat before her, fully erect, as she pulled my pants down to my ankles.

I heard a soft pant of delight as she bit the bottom of her lip.

"May I taste you?" she begged—sincerely begged.

No. Just tell her no. It's one thing to allow a hand job, but to allow her teeth so close to—

"Yes," I said.

"Thank you, Master," she said, licking her lips. A second later, I felt her hot breath surrounding me. My hips lifted to fill her warm mouth as her tongue dragged up and down my shaft. I knew I should have been nervous, that I was risking everything by letting this pet's lips on me, but she felt too good. This was highly dangerous, which was probably why it was also such a turn-on. For a moment, I got to feel like a normal guy, with a normal woman who wanted to please me—not because she had to, but because she *wanted* to.

As she bobbed her head up and down my length, her hands joined in on the action, massaging my shaft and my balls in such a delightful way that it made me see stars.

"Ah, Amanda!" I shouted, grabbing onto her hair as I thrust myself between her lips. She moaned in pleasure. She surprised me, then, by pulling away from me to remove the t-shirt I'd given her. Those perfect tits bobbed gently in front of me, nipples pebbled and begging to be touched. Unable to help myself, I cupped one of them, squeezing it gently. Our eyes locked as she moved one of her hands down to the lining of her panties.

"May I, Master?"

She wanted to play with herself. *Fuck.* I gave her another nod and watched as she fingered herself her eyes closing briefly with pleasure. "I need to taste you again, Connor. Please."

She'd used my name. Not "Master"—*Connor*. My hips bucked their approval as she went down on me again. As her mouth worked my cock, her right hand worked herself into a frenzy. Her mouth felt so good riding up and down my length that there was no way I could hold back my orgasm. I exploded against her tongue and she cried out in delight, swallowing me down with zero hesitation or disgust.

Panting, I held myself inside her dangerous lips longer than I should have, before pulling myself free. Amanda rocked back onto her heels and leaned against the coffee table. Her eyes watched me as I watched her, rubbing her clit in fast round circles. Her hips bucking against her own touch. Never had I witnessed one of the pets finish themselves off. Which told me I'd made her horny. I watched in rapt fascination until she screamed out and shook against her hand until her body relaxed and she removed her fingers, still damp with her wetness. It was the sexiest thing I'd ever seen.

Fuck. That was stupid. Not only had I let her suck me off, but I'd also let her get her kicks off too. She couldn't have that much power. I needed to put her back in her spot and remind her that she meant nothing to me outside of the paycheck she'd bring. Accordingly, I reached down and pulled my pants back on. "We have a busy day today. You and I are going to a party tomorrow to meet your possible owner." I made the mistake of looking at her. If I didn't know better, I would've thought she looked hurt by the thought of me getting rid of her.

No. She's a pet. Nothing more.

I shook my head. "This is a fast turnaround for any foster. I'm used to having weeks, or months if I need them, to get a pet ready for adoption, but time being what it is, we only have today to get you ready. That means you'll be with me all day." I looked down at my watch. It was already 9:15 a.m. "We have less than twenty-four hours to make you too good to pass up, which means there's no time to waste." I reached down and picked up the ankle monitor. "Put your foot on the table."

Amanda looked at me, and then at my hand. I expected her to shrink away, to run, scream, or, at the very least, verbally resist the order—all things a new pet would do. Instead, she surprised me, and put her ankle on the table. "Yes, Master."

Clenching my jaw, I secured the monitor on her foot. Its

blinking light assured me that it was secure. When it was on, I moved her foot back to the floor. "Do you know what this is?"

She nodded.

"Tell me."

"It's an ankle monitor. Sam had to wear one for six months when he was on house arrest once."

"Correct. The only difference is that with my monitor, if you step foot out of the parameters I've set, it doesn't alert the authorities. It alerts me, and my team—a team that has no issues taking the life of the foot it's attached to. Is that understood?"

She swallowed. It was clear she was scared, as she should be. My team would attempt to recover the asset unharmed first, but if I gave the order to terminate it, they would have zero hesitation in carrying it out. Fear was an appropriate response to the situation she was in.

"Understood, Master."

"Amanda, it is imperative that you follow my instructions. You have within your grasp the opportunity to get out of this cage," I said, gesturing to the unit. "You could get adopted this weekend and never have to see me again. The owner I have my eyes set on for you would treat you well, far better than any other fosters I've seen. You would be a fool to miss this chance. Most owners are cruel to their pets, but Malcolm wouldn't be—at least, I don't think so. He doesn't seem the type. This is your best shot at as normal a life as you can have. Selling you to Malcolm would be a gift."

"Thank you, Master."

I held her gaze, and for the first time since I had started this business, I secretly wished she would defy me, would make a run for it and piss off the buyer—anything so I wouldn't have to sell her off.

So I could keep her with me longer.

AMANDA

Connor's dark blue eyes seemed to be boring a hole through me, trying to find a crack in my façade. I couldn't let him see behind the mask. If a blow job and an ankle monitor could get me even one step closer to being out of this place, I was going to do everything in my power to comply. I wasn't foolish enough to think that Connor was giving me a line. I believed wholeheartedly that this Malcolm guy might be my Golden Ticket, the sort of guy I might be able to get to see reason and set me free—or one I could escape from. Staying here meant nothing but torture and fear. I would do everything Connor said so that when I was out of this hellhole, I'd be ready to run.

And ready to kill this son of a bitch.

There was only one problem. That blow job? I had enjoyed giving it, and I normally didn't. What was worse, when I had played with myself, I'd been genuinely aroused by him. My orgasm wasn't fake—I'd gotten off just looking at him.

Not cool.

My mind was playing a very dangerous game with my libido. I had to remember that Connor wasn't an object of desire, but one of fear. I couldn't be stupid about my next moves.

"Come," he said, tossing me back the t-shirt. I slipped it on. Once I was covered, he held out his hand. "Our work begins now."

I looked down at his hand. Having no choice, I accepted it, fighting to resist the warmth as it surrounded mine. He tugged me gently toward the door.

He was letting me out?

"I keep a unit a few doors down for weeks when I need to be more hands-on with my pets," Connor said. With one hand on the doorknob, his other came up to my throat. "While you may be tempted to make a run for it," he warned, "don't forget that your sensor will go off the moment you leave this floor. I have a fully-staffed lobby and drivers parked outside at all times. Any one of them will take you down, unless they hear otherwise from me."

I could only assume that he wasn't bluffing. Escape, at this point, was clearly not a viable option. Nodding, I held my emotions at bay. "I shall not leave your side, Master, unless instructed to do so."

He cocked his head and looked at me. *Shit.* Was I laying it on too thick?

"You've changed your tune since yesterday," he mused. "Yesterday, I was the devil, yet now, you allow me to hold your hand without a trace of fear behind those eyes. You're compliant and obedient. What game are you playing?"

Double shit. My eyes fell to the floor, terrified he'd see my panic. They weren't permitted to stay there long. Connor yanked my head up to look at him.

"I asked you a question. Why so compliant today? What changed?"

"You did," I said, thinking on the fly.

"How so?" He did not seem satisfied with my answer.

I bit my lip, stalling for time. "This morning, when you fell asleep beside me, I..." *I what?*

"Yes?" he pushed.

"I saw you differently." That wasn't exactly a lie. There had been a shift in me when I'd seen him there, an emotion other than fear.

"Different how, Amanda?"

"I don't know. I guess you looked sort of...beautiful. I wanted to fold you into my arms and never let you go," I said, hoping there was a shred of believability in my voice. I mean, he had looked different asleep. He hadn't looked cruel, then, but broken, and there had been a part of me that had wanted to heal him. When he slept, it was easier to see the man he could have been. "I know that sounds stupid," I added, "but it's the truth."

"Are you the Beauty to my Beast, then? Is that it?" Connor challenged. A slight curl of a smile danced on his lips.

"I don't have a yellow ballgown yet," I replied, as playfully as I could.

He surprised me by laughing. "I will give you this, Amanda—you're amusing." He opened the door to my cage, and I sucked in a breath. "Let's get you ready to meet your Prince Charming, shall we?"

The cool air from the hallway filled me with hope. I was one step closer to escaping. I'd find a way to get out of this, to free the other girls, then bury this man alive—even if it was the last thing I ever did.

CHAPTER THIRTEEN

Connor

Taking a pet out of its cage in its first week of captivity was unthinkable—hell, I didn't even like to do it before the first month. I required that a pet's spirit be thoroughly broken, their sense of hope shattered before I let them out, but this event at Malcolm's might be my only crack at selling Amanda to him. I needed to lord this sale over him—not only in retribution for how he'd price-gouged me when I'd bought this building, but also because he was one of the only men in town that I didn't have a leash on. That made him dangerous. Holding rich men's dirty laundry kept me safe, and so far, Malcolm's laundry was only stained. I needed it to be filthy.

That meant he needed to own one of my pets—balance the power scale. However, Malcolm was a bit of a recluse: he very rarely showed his face in public, and did his work in the shadows, which meant this party was the one chance I had to lure him with Amanda. For this to work, I needed to get her presentable and brainwashed enough to follow basic orders, fast. Every second would be essential for her training if this was to work. If I got my asking price, I might even be able to step out of my leadership role in the foster system, let my guys take over operations. It would be nice to not be looking over my shoulder all the time. Maybe I could have a semi-normal life for a change. One afternoon could turn my whole trajectory around.

"Do not let go of my hand, Amanda," I ordered, before leading her out to the hall. Not that she could get far even if she did try to run the second I opened the door, thanks to her ankle monitor and the thumbprint sensor in the elevator—but I was asserting my dominance. She needed to follow every order I gave her, no matter how small.

Amanda looked up at me with those gorgeous blue eyes, and I felt my heart rate kick into high gear. Her lips curled into a smile as she squeezed her hand against mine—willingly, without any hint of revulsion. "Yes, Master."

I flinched at the term, a first for me. I'd been called Master by my pets for years. Why did her saying it upset me? I shook the thought away.

"For now," I said, "I want you to call me Connor. This particular buyer is not like most. He must see you not as a puppet, ready to do anything he wishes, but as a partner. This buyer is unique, and will require me to train you differently than other pets. Is that understood?"

"Yes, Connor." She practically purred my name. Clenching my jaw, I lifted her chin upward, her eyes widening in shock at the sudden movement.

Good.

"If you are not adopted Saturday, you will revert to calling me Master, and be subject to normal foster training. You won't like that training, not one iota—so for your own sake, pay very close attention to my instructions, and you might prove to be my shortest foster ever."

She gave me a tense nod as I continued to hold her chin. It would be so easy to lean down and kiss her, claim her for my own, chain her to my bed, and leave Malcolm out of the equation. My thumb ran gently along her bottom lip.

No. Resist her.

Clenching my jaw, I let her face go. "My unit is right down the hall. It will do you no good to scream or run. I own the building: all of the doors are locked, and require my face to unlock them. The elevator is thumbprint-coded. Any attempt to make a run for it will only end in severe punishment."

"I won't run," Amanda said. I believed her.

"No, you won't, because until you're sold, *I* am your Master. Do what I say, and you'll live. If you don't, well...let's just say I have a bad temper."

She surprised me, then, by placing her other hand gently on my chest. "I won't leave your side."

A rush of emotion hit me. I wanted to pull her into my arms and keep her there forever. *No.* I couldn't risk that. She was a pet. A commodity. A paycheck. Nothing more.

"Good girl," I said, grasping her hand tight. I led her out into the hallway and locked her unit up. Then, I brought her to my door and did something reckless: I let her hand go. I had to know what she'd do. Would she make a run for it, even after all my warnings...or would she stay put? To my great surprise, Amanda slid her hand back inside mine.

What was going on in this woman's head that she would so willingly cling to the hand of her captor?

AMANDA

This was a test. I wasn't stupid. Connor was trying to see if I'd run.

The opportunity was right there—I could see the elevator. I could make it. But then what? Even if he was lying about the security he had in place, the odds of the elevator opening and closing before Connor's hands found my throat were impossible. Instead, I used the opportunity for recon. I made a mental note of how many doors there were on the floor: four on each side, eight per floor, thirteen floors. Over a hundred cages. This man knew what he was doing, and his threats weren't empty. This Malcolm guy might genuinely be my only legit escape plan, and I wasn't about to blow that by running.

"Very good, Amanda," he said, opening his unit. Just then, the elevator dinged, and I tensed. "Relax. It's the cleaners."

The doors opened and out came two large men in cleaning uniforms.

"Is it done?" Connor asked.

"This is the last load, sir."

"Very good. Thanks, gentlemen. If you can get the unit ready for another pet by the end of the day, there'll be a large bonus for you."

The taller of the men nodded. "Consider it done."

Connor smiled. "See? Nothing to be afraid of." He opened his door. "As long as you do everything I say." He let go of my hand and shoved me inside his apartment, closing the door swiftly behind him. "Sit on the couch, Amanda."

I nearly jumped at his order, but found myself hesitating. There were two black leather sofas opposite one another, with a large white fluffy rug in between them.

"Which one, Ma—Connor?" I asked, quickly correcting myself.

"Good girl—always better to clarify an order than to make an assumption," Connor replied. "That was a test, and you passed. The one on the left. Sit near the end table."

I did as instructed, crossing my ankles quickly. The more obedient he thought I was, the weaker he'd think I was. He'd be wrong on both counts, but I had to have a rock-solid plan first.

Connor walked to the end table and reached down, pulling out a drawer there. It was a unique table, seemingly made from steel, with a decorative metal pipe that ran around the perimeter. The pipe appeared worn and scratched, giving it a weathered look. "Place your hand on the armrest, Amanda."

Swallowing my fear, I put my hand on the edge of the couch. From the drawer, Connor pulled out a pair of handcuffs.

"I'm afraid this is necessary. My apartment is not pet-proof." He quickly secured my wrist in the cuff and the other to the metal pipe on the end table. "I call this Mjolnir," he explained. "Not even the God of Thunder himself could lift that table."

I didn't even try to escape. It was clear from the markings on the pipe that any attempt would be futile. I chose to save my strength.

"Kinky," I said, risking a look up at him.

Connor's eyes narrowed, and I wasn't sure if I'd pleased him or annoyed him. He was a hard man to read. He pulled out his phone from his back pocket, and started tapping the screen.

"What size dress do you wear? Six, eight?"

I felt myself frown. "Depends on the cut. I'm rather chesty, so sometimes I have to go a size or two up."

The glance he made down at my boobs was not lost on me. "Shoe size?"

"Seven and a half."

He nodded. "Date of your last menstrual cycle."

"Um...two weeks ago. Why?"

"So I know when to provide you with feminine hygiene products. I'm not uneducated in such matters." He typed more information into his phone. "Do you take any medications?"

"Just the pill when I can afford it, which lately isn't often."

Another nod. "I'll get you started on it Monday if you're not adopted by then. Any other health concerns your new master needs to know?"

I debated coming up with a list of things that would make me undesirable for "adoption," but I worried what the cost would be for either lying, or making myself appear useless for Connor's purposes.

"Amanda, I asked you a question."

"Sorry, no. Nothing. Healthy as a horse." Save for a little mental trauma.

He finished typing and slipped the phone back into his pocket. "Good. Now, first up, I need to find you some proper attire for Saturday's party. It will be a luncheon, probably outdoors if I know

Malcolm. He loves nature. But don't let that give you any ideas—you'll still have the tracker on your ankle.

"Won't people see it?" I asked, regretting it as soon as I said it.

He only laughed. "When I'm done with you, no one will be looking at your ankle—but no, I'm not worried about your monitor. I have just the boot for that." The smile Connor wore told me that he'd done this type of thing a lot. He had no doubt planned for every possible outcome. Still, I clung to the hope that, once I was out of this building, I'd find a way to escape. I needed to make it to Saturday. One step at a time.

"Stay here, pet. I'm about to get us some things to play with." He winked at me, then left me alone in his living room. What "things" did he mean—and, more importantly, what did he mean by "play?"

CHAPTER FOURTEEN

Connor

With Amanda secured to Mjolnir, I went into the stock room. The second bedroom of the unit was dedicated to all my pets' needs: clothing, linens (if they earned them), food, medications, etc. Since most of the pets I fostered were roughly the same body shape—guys had a type—it was easy to amass a collection of clothing for any need, including a Saturday brunch at Malcolm Luxx's mansion.

I'd been to his house once before: it had a sweeping floorplan, a patio, and a pool. The man had taste, I'd give him that. Because Malcolm liked his privacy, his outdoor area was highly-gated. Even if Amanda tried to run, she wouldn't get past those barriers—but just in case, I'd have one of my boys on standby in the neighborhood.

Sliding the garments along the rack, I frowned. Amanda couldn't wear a red-sequined, floor-length evening dress to a brunch, even though she had the figure to do the gown justice, more so than prior pets. However, for this brunch, I'd need something more restrained—suitable for fall weather, but still sexy.

I grabbed a few options, and was about to go back to Amanda, when my phone buzzed. A smile brushed my lips when I saw who it was.

"Morning, Malcolm. What can I do for you?"

"My assistant tells me that you'll be attending my birthday brunch."

"Yes, my girl said she was able to secure us a spot. Wouldn't want to miss such a momentous occasion for the world. It's your thirty-second, right?"

"Cut the shit, Connor. I know what you're up to, and I already told you, I'm not interested in 'fostering' a pet."

"I know what you've told me, Malcolm," I soothed. *You haven't met Amanda yet, though.*

There was a pause on the other end of the line. "I'm serious, Connor. I'm not interested."

Oh, but he would be. I suppressed a grin. "Understood. It's cool if *I* bring a pet though, right? One of my own?"

Malcolm scoffed. "You, a pet? I thought you didn't do that."

I shrugged and picked up a pair of tall black boots. "I don't. But you know what they say—sometimes a pet chooses you."

"Mm-hm. Whatever. Just as long as you aren't trying to shove her on me."

To my surprise, my jaw clenched a few times. "No, this one's mine. I might let you pet-sit her one day...but owning her? Out of the question." There was no hint of humor in my voice.

"Goodbye, Connor," Malcolm huffed.

Staring at my phone, I couldn't help but wonder if what I'd said to Malcolm had been a reverse psychology move to make him want what he couldn't have...or if I'd been serious. Was I *actually* considering keeping Amanda for myself?

No, that was too dangerous. Reckless. She had to go.

Grabbing a few hangers, I walked back into the living room. Amanda was exactly where I'd left her. Not that she could have gone anywhere if she wanted to. What was odd, however, was the look on her face. She seemed content. There was no fear in her eyes, no tension on the cuff. It was almost as though she felt comfortable here. With me.

"Was this how he taught you to behave when he entered a room?" I asked.

She blinked at me. "Who?"

"Samuel P. Banner. The ex. Did he teach you how to be so obedient?"

Amanda's jaw hardened, as if she was annoyed that I'd discovered her dirty little secret. "My father was my first teacher. Sam was a hack compared to him," she said, her eyes focused on something far away. A memory, maybe?

"Tell me." I leaned against the couch, draping the garments over the back. It was clear that she didn't want to talk about it, and I understood. Though she was in no position to defy me, I sensed her discomfort about bringing up something that was likely traumatizing.

"When I was six," Amanda began, "my father got into a car accident. It messed up his left arm pretty bad. He was in a lot of pain, and they gave him Oxy. This was back before they understood how addictive it was. When his doctor wouldn't refill his prescription anymore, he turned to the bottle."

"Ah, yes. I know that one. My dad is a drunk as well, and a sappy one at that—would constantly tell my mother that he loved her, that I was the best son in the world, then proceed to pass out for days at a time."

"You're lucky. Mine was a mean drunk," Amanda admitted. "Some days, I was almost envious of my mother's death. She got to escape so much hurt." Her voice trembled. "But I learned quickly that if I was complacent, if I didn't make a fuss, he would often forget I was in the room. Then, the state 'rescued' me, and it's been a joyride ever since."

"How old were you when they came?"

She closed her eyes and let out a breath. "Thirteen."

"That's young."

She shrugged. "I survived."

I nodded. She was strong, like me. "My mother used to lock me in a dog kennel when I displeased her...which was often." The truth had escaped my lips before I could stop it. It was too late to retract the words, so I leaned into it. "I could never seem to predict whether she would be happy with my actions, or punish me for them."

"She put you in a *dog kennel*?" The horror in Amanda's voice unsettled me.

"Often without food or any sort of creature comforts. So what I do here," I said, gesturing around, "is leaps and bounds better than what I grew up with. That's how I know how much can be endured—because I've survived worse."

"I'm sorry."

I glanced at her, then. She had a tear running down her cheek. It wasn't pity that lingered in her eyes, but understanding—a shared realization that both of our childhoods had been taken from us. It was no one's fault. It just *was*.

Shaking the memories away, I stood and held up the first dress. Time to shake off the frail boy I had been, and remember the man I'd become. "Let's try this one on for size."

Amanda's eyes went to the hanger that I was balancing on my finger. "How can I do that? I'm chained to a table."

Another pet would have been smacked for speaking without being spoken to, but there wasn't time for any bruises to heal, so I let it slide. It was also a valid question.

"It's poncho-style. It's open on the sides, and crosses over itself to tie in the back. Not my first rodeo." I winked. Setting the other selections down on the couch, I opened the neck of the dress and walked toward her. "Stand up."

Amanda did as she was told, though she had to hunch slightly, as the cuff limited how much she could move. She reached for the dress, but I stopped her. "The shirt I gave you needs to come off, first."

Her cheeks reddened, and it made my dick twitch.

"Right," she said, reaching down to grab the bottom of the fabric.

"Allow me," I replied. Reaching into my back pocket, I pulled out a pocketknife. The blade was sharp and strong enough to gut a deer, a weapon I carried with me at all times. You never knew when you'd need to gut something.

I took a step forward so that our bodies were almost touching, and slid the blade easily through the shirt I'd given her. When it reached the neckline, I paused and made the mistake of looking into Amanda's eyes. They were on mine, full of desire—not even an ounce of fear.

Only need.

I pushed the blade under the neckline and pulled hard until it went through. I tugged against the fabric one last time, leaving Amanda standing, once again, in only her panties. Her lips parted, and a small gasp escaped her as the fabric fell at her feet.

I took a step back and looked at her. She swallowed hard, but she wasn't scared. She was turned on, and her arousal excited me. Without a second thought, I placed the blade against Amanda's ribcage. She sucked in a breath, causing her breasts to rise. *Damn, she was sexy.*

Dragging the edge of the blade slowly up her side and around to the front, I slid the tip underneath the curve of her breast. Amanda's breath rose and fell with anticipation. She was radiant. Never had I laid eyes on a woman so breathtaking. A guttural sound escaped my lips as I took in her perfection. Her nipples peaked, eager and waiting to be suckled. She arched her back, practically begging my lips to caress them. I felt myself growing hard. One thought crossed my mind as looked back at her waiting lips: *Mine.*

Unable to resist those luscious curves, I lowered my mouth to one of her breasts. My tongue encircled her nipple, sucking and pulling it gently. As much as I wanted to cup her other breast, I wasn't about to let go of the knife. I might be aroused, but I wasn't stupid. Instead, I traced the tip of the blade down her back until I reached her panties. A moment later, that barrier was also gone. I wanted to see all of her. Taste her.

Pulling my lips off her breast, I took a step back to look at my prize. She stood naked before me, beautiful and bare. I had never been more attracted to a woman in my entire life.

"Sit down," I ordered.

She bit the edge of her bottom lip, but quickly complied. I placed the knife on the arm of the other couch, well out of her grasp, but left the blade out just in case.

"Are you going to cut me?" she asked.

I smirked. She had the intelligence to not trust the monster, but her eyes told me a different story—she was as turned on as I was. "Not unless you give me cause."

"Then what *are* you going to do to me?" she asked. No, *begged*.

"Pleasure you," I said, sinking to my knees. "Now, spread your legs."

AMANDA

Under normal circumstances, a date with a man putting the moves on me like this would've been stupidly hot. There was something quite sexy about a man taking something he wanted from his compliant partner.

But that was the sticking point—I *wasn't* compliant, not really. I had to pretend to be, had to play the game if I wanted to make it out of here. Sam had taught me well how to act aroused in the face of danger. The more I'd seemed turned on by him, the less he'd hit me. But it was a balance. He hadn't liked it if he thought I was acting. Those were the worst beatings—when I'd "tricked" him. I couldn't risk a failed performance with Connor. Sam might've given me a black eye, or ten, but I had no doubt Connor wouldn't flinch at skinning me alive. His leaving the knife in plain sight, out of my reach, was all the reminder that I needed.

Knowing any hesitation on my part could be potentially mean my demise. I quickly spread my legs apart. While my father or Sam had hurt me enough to put me in my place, now there was hesitation about whether my value as a sale would outweigh Connor's temper if I were to test him. I wouldn't be able to save the other girls if I was dead. I had to give him *exactly* what he wanted.

"Wider."

I struggled with how his command sent a shiver through me. *No, Amanda, do not enjoy this.* Pushing down my desire, I locked eyes with him and did as he instructed, opening myself up as far as I could go.

"Good girl," he said, crawling over to me on his hands and knees. It shouldn't have been so hot. He was holding me against my will. I was laid out bare to him, at his command, and I was wet. *Fuck.*

As his lips found the top of my knee, I wondered, for a moment, if my thighs had enough power enough to crush him. Considering I hadn't hit a gym in forever, I knew I'd never have the strength able to hold him long, let alone choke him, and even if I did, where would I go? I was still handcuffed, still locked inside a building with 24/7 surveillance. If he didn't get me, someone else would. No, I had to play this smart. I had to let Connor be in control, had to let him think he held the power.

"I've never been with a true redhead before," he said, his thumbs running up my inner thighs. My skin prickled with gooseflesh at the unexpected sensation.

"Once you try me," I cooed, scooting myself closer to the edge, ready to hurry up and get this over with, "you'll never want another."

Connor's thumbs froze mere inches from my core. *Shit, did I blow it? Did he know I was acting?*

His eyes found mine and held me there. "And what would you do if that proved to be true? What if I tasted your garden and decided not to sell you, but, instead, kept you here with me forever —using you to please my every waking whim?"

He wouldn't, would he? No. I was worth more to him as a sale.

He was saying that to mess with my mind, trying to test my loyalty.

"You're a tease," I said. I arched my back, seeming to beg him to return to me. But that wasn't what I wanted...Was it?

"Fuck me, you're sexy," he growled—like, a literal fucking *growl*. A moment later, he buried his face between my thighs. I let out a gasp as his tongue slipped inside me. Without my consent, my body betrayed me, my hips rocking upward to meet him, urging him to find my clit.

Amanda, this guy kidnapped you. He's going to sell you! What the hell are you doing, enjoying his touch? My head tipped back, unable to hear reason—only desire. I let out a moan of delight as Connor worked his magic on me, all rational thought disappearing like a mist.

With my hips slightly off the couch, his hands cupped my ass, digging into my skin, his fingertips pulling me closer to him. Despite my best efforts to remain in control, to shut my emotions off, I couldn't. I needed to feel this. His tongue was magical, hitting me in all the right places.

"Holy shit," I cried out. He was amazing at this. I was so turned on that I couldn't keep my hips from rising to meet his every move. The way he licked, and sucked, and applied exactly the right pressure made my head spin. He could cut me now, and I wouldn't even care. I was so close.

My cries seemed to spur something in Connor. He worked me faster, harder, needing no direction. His hands moved from my back and anchored itself to my hip. One hand kept my hips right where he wanted them, while his other hand squeezed my breasts in time with his mouth. I lost all logic, forgetting about who this man was, about my situation.

All that mattered was my release.

With my free hand, my fingers twined into the blonde locks at the nape of his neck, pushing him deeper into my core. I was so close. *So close*.

"Connor, please," I panted.

He lifted himself for a moment. "Please, what? What do you want, Amanda?"

My answer horrified me. "You. All of you, Connor. Inside me. Now."

Sitting back on his heels he looked at me, almost as if he were doubting my motives.

"Please," I begged again, "I need to feel you inside of me." And here was the worst part: I did. It wasn't an act. I *wanted* him to fuck me.

Suddenly, Connor stood up, and I worried if I'd said something wrong. Then, his hands went to his belt, where he made quick work of removing his pants, clothes pooling at his feet. My God, he was beautiful. And hard. For me.

His hands clasped my hips and he started to turn me around, wanting to take me from behind. Then, he seemed to change his mind. Our eyes locked.

"Are you sure?" Connor asked. There was a genuine hesitancy in his voice, making me wonder if he was as conflicted about this as I was.

"Positive," I replied. "Please, I need you."

With a pinched brow, Connor lowered himself onto the couch, my legs still spread wide for him, core wet and ready. I wanted him, *needed* him inside of me. It was both disturbing and arousing at the same time. I watched with desire as he lined himself up to my seam. He looked up at me, and I pressed my hand against his hips, guiding him forward. A moment later, he was inside me.

I let out a shriek of pleasure as he filled me. It was heaven. My fingers dug into his skin, pulling him towards me. He seemed to resist, not wanting to be too close, but I couldn't stop trying to bring him to me.

"Connor, yes, that's so good," I moaned against his ear.

He didn't say anything for several moments, slowly moving in and out of me. Then, without warning, his lips were on mine. Hard and urgent kisses. Our tongues danced around each other's, our hips syncing up. Being chained, I wasn't able to hold him the way I wanted to, but I held onto him as tightly as I could with my free hand, wanting to feel more and more of his touch.

Connor pulled his lips off mine and pressed his forehead to my neck. "Fuck, I'm going to cum," he said, trying to pull out.

No fucking way. I was too close. My legs looped around his hips, caging him in place, as he thrust against me. The smack of our skin in combination with his sudden grunt of release, set me over the edge. I came around his cock.

Drenched in sweat and semen, we lay there awkwardly on the couch, Connor's length still inside of me, panting our way back to normalcy.

What the hell was that?

That, Amanda, was the best sex of your life...and it just so happened to be with your kidnapper.

This was not good. Not good *at all*.

CHAPTER FIFTEEN

Connor

With my dick still inside Amanda, I pinched my eyes closed, trying to come to terms with what had just happened.

I'd fucked pets countless times. That was nothing new. It was part of the housebreaking process. They needed to submit to their new owner's demands at the drop of a hat, and it was part of my job to train them to bow to my will.

What *was* new, however, was that I hadn't taken Amanda from behind. I had faced her while entering her, had let her look me in the eyes, had kissed her on the mouth—and, even more disturbingly, had eaten her out. I'd never done that for a pet. What did it matter to me if they got any satisfaction from my actions? A pet's desires were of no interest to me, nor would they be to an owner. But with Amanda, I had found myself unable to resist tasting her. I had wanted to make sure she got off, had needed to know that *I* was making her feel good. My own needs had been secondary—a definite first.

Of course, Amanda had no idea about any of this. For all she was aware, I'd fucked her brains out just as I did with all of the pets, nothing more. And while the sex has been great, maybe even the best of my life, I couldn't let her know that it had been anything special...mostly because I couldn't deal with the fact that it might have meant more than I was ready to admit.

As much as I didn't want to, I withdrew myself from her, and stood up.

"Here," I said, bending down to pick up the torn shirt I'd cut off her. "You can clean yourself up with this."

Amanda took the shirt with a strange look, almost as if she was upset that I'd left her side. *Good.* I needed to make her think that what had happened between us was nothing, because that's what she needed to be to me: nothing. Relationships were not allowed in my world. They were little more than a liability. Even with my father, I went to great lengths to shelter our connection for his own protection. There were many who would love to see me hurt for what I'd done to them, and would have no issue slicing up my father. He may have been a gambling drunk, but he was my blood —and, like it or not, my mother had loved him. So I did what I could.

I left Amanda on the couch while I went to clean up in the shower. Once the water was running in my sink, I tried to screw my head back on straight. If what just happened was any indication, I needed to sell her ASAP—if not to Malcolm, then to the next highest bidder. I might not even finish her housetraining if I could unload her fast enough. Hell, if it came to it, I'd call Vincent to take her off my hands. He had his own setup in Mexico, but I didn't see him as a competitor. His women were used for other purposes. I didn't ask questions. We respected each other's businesses in that way. Sure, he was much harsher on his women, but I couldn't risk Amanda getting under my skin. It was too risky.

One way or the other, she would be off my hands by Monday. Already, I felt lighter.

After I dried myself off, I called Vincent to let him know what might be coming down the line for him. I'd arrange for Amanda's transportation over the border, naturally, but I'd need his thumbs-up before I sent her packing. He answered on the fourth ring, an idiosyncrasy of his: he'd answer on the fourth ring, or not at all.

"Connor, my man. What's good?" I could practically taste the cigar he was likely puffing on. Vincent was rarely seen without one, and judging by the rasp in his voice, it was a practice he'd started as a teen. While Vincent was only in his late thirties, he had the voice of someone twice that.

"Listen," I started, "I might have a pet I need to get off my hands Monday. I'm meeting with a potential owner this weekend, but if that falls through, I'll need to unload her. I don't have the kennel space." The lie came easily, not that I owed him one.

"Um...I might be able to help you out. Got any more deets you can send over?"

"I'll have her adoption papers delivered to your US contact by the end of the day. He can provide you the details."

"Yeah, yeah. Good."

It would have been faster to send him the files digitally, but Vincent preferred communication that could be shredded. His put is trust in his people, not technology. Glancing toward where I'd left Amanda, I nodded my head. "I'll let you know by Sunday evening if I need to offload her."

"Assuming I like what I see. No guarantees, man."

He'd like Amanda. What wasn't to like? "Understood."

Hanging up with him, I slipped on some new gray sweats and yanked on a white t-shirt. I printed off Amanda's specs, slipped them into a courier envelope, and set up a time for pick up. Patricia was off today, so that meant I'd need to leave it in our delivery box in the lobby.

Walking back into the living room, I stopped short. Amanda was still sitting naked on the couch. I'd momentarily forgotten she was here. I forced my eyes away from her body.

"I think it's safe to assume the dress I have for Malcolm's party will fit." I picked the hanger up and glanced back at her glorious figure. "I'll get you something else to put on for now."

Snagging the rest of the dresses from where I'd draped them over the couch, I went back to the closet to hang them up. Then, I found Amanda a pair of navy blue sweats and an oversized hoodie.

They were several sizes too big for her, which would make her look frumpy—exactly what I needed. That should cool my hormones down.

When I got back into the living room, I tossed the clothes at her and told her to get dressed. She fumbled getting the pants on, but wasn't able to do the hoodie because she was still cuffed.

"I'm going to uncuff you so that you can get dressed," I said, "but if you make a move to run or harm me, I'll have my knife in your abdomen faster than you can reach the door. Is that understood?"

Amanda merely nodded, holding the balled-up hoodie in front of her tits. Probably for the best—seeing her naked was not doing me any favors.

"Eyes on the floor," I ordered.

She quickly complied, while I went to the kitchen to retrieve the key from its hidden spot under the stove vent. Walking back to her, told her to sit while I straddled her waist, pinning her down. She sucked in a breath as my weight settled on top of her, and I resisted the urge to kiss those quivering lips.

"Do not disappoint me by doing something stupid," I warned.

Her big eyes found mine and, somehow, I sensed she would obey me—not because she feared me, but because she wanted to. She *wanted* to do whatever I instructed her to.

Or maybe that was all in my head.

Moving my hand down Amanda's arm, I slowly turned the key to let her out—realizing, at that exact moment, that I hadn't put the knife back in my pocket.

AMANDA

The thing about gray sweatpants that men didn't understand was that they acted like a wet T-shirt—allowing onlookers to see every lump and bump.

Or, in this case, lack thereof.

No, not his cock—that was *definitely* visible, one massive specimen—but the lump missing from Connor's right pocket. The knife wasn't on him. From the corner of my eye, I could see it still sitting open across from me, its blade glinting in the sunlight, mere feet from my grasp.

I had about ten seconds to decide if I had enough physical strength to shove him off me and sink the knife into him before he could snag it first. Even if I did somehow manage to get the knife...what then? Could I *really* kill Connor? If I did, I would still need his thumbprint to get out of his apartment, maybe even his retinal scan to get out of the building—I'd have to hack his body into bits. Not to mention the ankle monitor I still had on. I might somehow escape the building, but for how long? He had to have security cameras, back-up plans, hired thugs that would shoot first and ask questions later.

No, I couldn't risk it. Any attempt to escape now would only result in my suffering or my death, and then, there would be no hope for the others trapped. I was in a unique position, and I couldn't rush it—I had to give this plan time to work. Connor had to trust me. I had to learn more about how the building was set up, and how he ran things, if I ever wanted to escape and save the others.

Given no choice, I did the only thing I could do: I obeyed Connor's orders and held perfectly still while he released me from the cuffs. As soon as they were off, his hand was around my neck in a vice-grip, pinning me to the couch. He thought I would run.

"I'm not going to try and escape," I choked out. *Not yet.* Connor released some of the pressure so that I could breathe again, but he kept his hand where it was. Taking a giant gamble, I placed my free hand on his chest. "Why would I run?"

His eyes darted down to where I had placed my palm over his heart. His eyebrows pinched tightly together as he glared at my hand.

"What are you doing?" he hissed.

I moved my hand away, stung. "I don't know. I'm sorry, I just..."

"You just what?"

"I—I wanted to touch you. I acted before I thought about it. I'm sorry." I forced my eyes to the floor.

For a moment, he didn't say anything. His body was crushing mine into the couch, and I watched his chest rise and fall. Eventually, his nostrils flared.

"You don't think I know what you're doing?" Connor asked. He moved his hand off my neck to pinch my jaw instead, forcing my eyes up to his. I wanted to respond, but I couldn't. He looked so angry. "You're not the first, Amanda, to try and manipulate me into caring about you. I don't—got it? I'm not some weak guy you can manipulate with a pouty lip. You can't make me fall for you. I can't love anyone. I don't have a heart."

There was something in the way he said that last sentence that almost sounded like regret. I used it to my advantage, looking him dead in the eye.

"Neither do I."

He let me go, then, and for a split second, his mask slipped. I could see the hurt boy behind the hardened eyes of time. I knew the look because I had it, too. You recognize trauma when you see it in others.

And that realization made him the tiniest bit more human.

"You don't know anything about me, Amanda." He stood up and grabbed the knife from off the other couch and held it out, pointing it right at my heart. "Never assume that you do. Is that understood?"

I nodded my compliance, not daring to push my luck. But one thing was certain: I'd rattled him. My plan was working. I was getting under his skin—and, like it or not, he was getting under mine.

Eventually, Connor lowered the knife, closed it, and put it in his pocket. He watched me for several minutes, but I didn't budge from my spot. Clearly, he was trying to process something, and I didn't want to interrupt him.

"I need to run downstairs to drop off a package," he said after a moment. "Since we're against the wall with training, I'm going to give you *one* chance to prove to me that you can venture out to see Malcolm. Trust me, you do not want to blow this test: Malcolm will be a hell of a lot kinder than the man I'll sell you to if you fail me."

My heart started to race. That was all I wanted—his trust. So that I could manipulate it.

"I'm going to leave you here, in my apartment, without the cuffs. You are to sit on that couch and wait for my return. You are not to lift a single ass cheek off the leather. Understood?"

I nodded once. I wasn't about to fail.

Connor took one deep breath, then picked up a manila envelope and his cell phone, and left me in his apartment. Alone. My gut was screaming at me to get up and find a weapon, an escape, a phone—*something* to get out of this situation—but my brain knew better. If my unit was under surveillance, I would bet my ass his was too. He'd be watching my every move. The envelope probably wasn't even real. He just wanted to know what I'd do when I thought I wasn't being watched. But I wasn't stupid. I knew there were cameras on me even now—that's why he felt safe to leave. He had given up zero control. There was no risk for him. This was *my* test to fail. But I wasn't going to.

Let him watch. I wasn't running.

Not *yet*.

CHAPTER SIXTEEN

Connor

Closing the door behind me, I stood in the hall and pulled up the screen outside the door to watch what Amanda would do. The image came to life and showed me that she was still on the couch, no doubt listening for the coast to be clear.

I waited. I watched. A full three minutes passed, and she just sat there: legs crossed, hands in her lap.

Interesting.

Switching to my phone, I pulled up the unit's camera so I could monitor her. Being sure not to make any noise, I walked down the hall and to the elevator, cursing the ding that came with its arrival. That was probably what she'd been waiting for—now she'd make her move. When the doors closed, I watched the video. Any second now, Amanda would try to run.

Yet she didn't. She sat still. If she hadn't reached up to scratch an itch, I would have assumed the feed was on a loop.

"What are you up to?" I asked as the elevator descended.

I reached the lobby, but there was still no movement from Amanda. Making quick work of the drop-off, I got back in the elevator, and that was when she finally moved. I braced myself to see what she'd try first. The door? The kitchen to search for a knife? I wasn't prepared, however, when she didn't move to get off the couch. Instead, Amanda reached down and picked something up off the seat beside her.

The shirt I'd cut off her. Odd choice. Was she going to try and choke me with it? She'd never have the strength. Then, Amanda did something unfathomable—she brought the balled-up fabric to her nose, closed her eyes, and inhaled deeply. When she lowered the shirt, she was smiling. Did my scent please her? She took another deep inhalation before she balled up the fabric and pressed her face against it, clinging to it like one might a lover.

Odd.

The elevator doors opened, and I continued to watch the screen. Amanda must have heard the elevator, because she quickly took one last sniff of the shirt, then tossed it back to the side where it had been before. I unlocked the apartment door without ordering her to sit, because I knew she was where she was supposed to be.

Locking us in, I looked at Amanda. "You obeyed my orders." I tried to hide the shock in my voice, but it betrayed me. "Why didn't you try to run?"

I walked over to the sofa and sat across from her, peering deeply into her eyes to catch her in a lie.

"You told me not to get off the couch, so I didn't."

"Yes, I know what I told you, but I'm surprised you listened. Most don't so early in their training."

She shrugged. "I guess I'm not like the others."

"No, you are not," I conceded. I nodded at the shirt on the couch. "One more question— why did you smell my shirt?"

Amanda's eyes widened, as though she only now realized that she'd been watched. "I..." she sputtered.

"Yes?" I pushed. "The truth, Amanda. I'll know if you're lying."

Eyes glued to the floor, she fiddled with her fingers. "I like how you smell."

She looked up, then, gaze locking with mine. Against my better judgment, I felt myself smile. "Well, don't get used to it. If all goes well, you'll be out of my hair soon."

Her eyes left mine to focus on the edge of the coffee table. She looked almost...dejected.

"Come, we have lots of work to do." I stood up and held out a hand to her. She looked at my outstretched palm and hesitated, but only for a second, before sliding her thin hand easily into mine —as if it was made to be there.

Shaking my head to clear my thoughts, I led her into my room...a place no pet had ever been allowed access to. I walked her over to my desk and powered up my laptop. Pulling out the office chair, I sat down, then pulled Amanda onto my lap, caging her in my arms. I needed her where I could see her, since she was uncuffed. Her hair brushed the side of my face as she leaned against my chest, and I felt myself rising to meet her touch. Grinding my teeth, I forced myself to focus.

"I need to give you a crash course on your potential new master," I began. "His name is Malcolm Luxx. He's in a similar line of business as me—not trading in humans, but valuable works of art. Stolen art, to be exact, though he doesn't want anyone to know it's stolen. He'll be turning thirty-two on Saturday, and you are to be his present, if he'll have you."

I felt her head turn to look at me, but I kept my eyes focused on pulling up the right documents. I couldn't let her being this close to me become a distraction.

"Malcom's resistant to the idea of adopting a pet—he thinks it's inhumane—but I think he'll be unable to say no to you." I turned to look at her, then, her gaze hovering on my lips. I felt an overwhelming urge to lean over and kiss her, to throw her on the bed and take her once again, but I blinked myself back into reality. Everything but Malcom's picture was up on the screen. He was a bit of a recluse, and getting photos of him had proven challenging. Not that I needed one. I knew who he was. Everyone in the underworld was aware of what one another was doing—it was how we were able to survive so long. Everyone kept everyone else's secrets, so that we could all continue to play, and those that ratted others out didn't live long. It was best to keep to your own business affairs.

Nodding at the screen, I let out a breath. "All of the data I've collected on Malcolm over the years has led me to believe that a buxom redhead might be his fetish. That's why you were chosen, Amanda, from the long list of rental applicants for that unit—you fit the profile to perfection."

Amanda's eyes went from the screen back to me. "And what if he doesn't want me? Do I return here with you?"

There was an undeniable whisper of hope in her voice, hope I couldn't afford for her to hold onto.

"No. If Malcolm is not interested, you'll be sent to another buyer, one far crueler than I am. He will take you out of the country, and you will become a ghost. Malcolm is your best shot at a life outside of a literal cage—Vincent uses actual dog kennels, worse than the one I was kept in. You have one chance to make Malcolm want you. *One.* Do you understand your situation?"

Amanda looked up at me with those big puppy-dog eyes. "I need to seduce Malcolm," she said. I hated how that sounded on her lips. "But either way, you'll be rid of me."

Was that regret in her voice?

I had to pull away from her stare. It was too intense.

"Correct," I replied. "Normally, you would have spent longer here, but this situation is unique. At least Malcolm is conventionally handsome. Most of my clients aren't."

My fingers touched a few buttons on the keyboard, cycling between files. "He's about my height, and seems to prefer a slight beard, at least in the photos I've been able to procure. He's rich, obviously, because my services are not cheap, which means he's a professional. He's also intelligent and notoriously private. The party he's hosting is the only event most people see him at, and the guest list is highly-pruned. He trusts no one, which makes him smarter than most. You have this one night to sell your 'assets' because he will resist you. The bastard has morals, even though he's a bloody thief." I shook my head at the irony. "He doesn't approve of my stealing women, but he has no issues stealing other artists' talent. Hypocrite. Still, he has the money I want, money I'm *owed*, so you need to make damn sure he's willing to pay whatever price I demand."

I found myself moving my fingers off the keyboard to wrap around her waist, pressing her body to mine, almost as though I was repulsed by the idea of Malcolm taking her. I caught the hitch of her breath as I pressed her to me, saw the way her chest was rising and falling in rapid succession—as if she was affected by how close my lips had suddenly gotten to hers.

Jesus, was I about to kiss her?

Clearing my throat, I loosened my grip and finally moved one of my hands away, bringing it back to the keyboard. The other one still held onto her—in case she ran, I rationalized.

"Malcolm is believed to be an introvert, so even though this will be a party for him, we likely won't see him for long. Our window will be narrow, but he'll have cameras. He's as careful as I am. He'll make the connections he needs to make, and then he'll disappear. Once we're on his property, you'll need to be on your A-game—you'll never know if he's watching or not, so your first impression will be crucial."

I looked up at her and caught Amanda scanning the screen, but there was no security threat—she'd never be in a position to use this information for anything. If she was trying to memorize facts or dates, she'd soon realize that was a wasted effort.

"What's his type?" Amanda asked, not seeming to find what she was looking for on the screen. Instead, she focused her navy-blue eyes on me. Malcolm wouldn't stand a chance against those eyes.

I let out a deep sigh. "Honestly, I don't know. I don't get the sense that he's looking for a trophy wife, or anything too sexually wild, but it's hard to know. He's so private—he could be into all sorts of grotesque things. My gut tells me to be yourself. Malcolm would probably see through you otherwise."

She let out a small breath. "I'm not exactly sure who *I* am." Her fingers twined together again, a nervous tick.

"You're a bit too young to have an identity crisis," I teased.

"Am I? I mean, isn't the person I thought I was essentially gone? Now that I'm a 'pet,' what autonomy do I have except to bow to a billionaire's will? I think that calls for some level of an identity crisis."

I shrugged. "There are worse ways to live."

"I know," Amanda whispered. "I've been there. Done that." She shivered against some memory. "I know how perverted men can be, Connor, but those moments in their beds...at least I was warm. And a lot of times, I got dinner first. I'm used to being good for what my body can do for men."

My jaw clenched listening to her talk. My research hadn't dug up that part of her past, just the last few years of her life. Usually, that's all I needed to go on. It sounded like Amanda had had it nearly as rough as I had.

"And that led you to Sam?" I asked.

She nodded. "I was stupid. I fell for his lies, thought he loved me, or at least *liked* me. Now, I realize that's how predators work: they lure you in with a false sense of security, get you dependent on their 'generosity,' and then comes the abuse when you don't live up to their expectations." She shifted in my lap. "This may sound crazy, but being held captive...it's not all bad. I have a bed. It's warm. There's enough food that I won't starve. There is some level of care, even if it's only to protect an investment."

Amanda let out a heavy sigh, and without even thinking about it, my arms wrapped around her, wanting to take some of her shame away. She flinched at first—I did, too, if I was being honest —but then she leaned into me, and I felt the weight of her against my chest. Hugging people was not in my nature. I couldn't even recall if I had ever been hugged, if I were honest. Yet, with her in my arms, it seemed natural. Soothing. Like I never wanted to let her go. That was a problem.

AMANDA

As Connor held me in his arms, I could hear my heart beating wildly. I couldn't tell if it was from the fear that he might hurt me, or the fear that he might see my desire and kiss me, but I decided to use that fear to my advantage.

"Can you tell how hard my heart is beating right now?" I whispered. Connor moved one of his hands off my waist and brought it up to my chest. His palm rested inches above my breast, feeling for my heartbeat.

"You're scared of me. Good. You should be," he said, pushing me off his lap and stepping away from the chair.

"No...I'm not scared," I replied. "It just happens. You walk in the room, and I have instant heart palpitations. You arouse me. I can't help it." Though it wasn't exactly a lie, it was misleading—I *was* scared of Connor, but I was also oddly attracted to him.

A second later, Connor's hand was around my throat.

He stood up and pushed me against the wall, hard. My head smacked loudly against the drywall, and for a moment, I saw stars. I froze, watching Connor's eyes narrow into dangerous slits, and realized in that moment, far too late, that he held the power to kill me. It wasn't a power play—he could literally squeeze the life out of me right now, and no one would ever come looking for me. I'd been reckless, and now I might pay the ultimate price.

Connor's grip on my neck didn't loosen for a moment. "Do not get comfortable with me, woman," he snarled. "I am not your boyfriend, I am not your savior, and I'm sure as hell not your protector." He shoved me again, causing my head to hit the wall once more. "I am your master until I can unload you for a price. *That* is all you are to me—an item to sell. Never forget that."

My fingers clawed against his hand, trying to escape his death grip. Tears welled in my eyes as the air ran out, then I gasped for breath as Connor finally let me go. Coughing, I collapsed to the floor at his feet.

So much for my seduction skills.

CHAPTER SEVENTEEN

Amanda

The stars were still dancing around my head from when Connor had nearly sent me through the drywall. Clearly, I'd pushed my luck trying to get too close to him. I was lucky he hadn't killed me for trying to play him like that.

I tried not to move from where I had landed, another lesson learned from trial and error: do nothing to bring any attention to yourself. Try to disappear.

Usually, the abuser would move to a different room, then, disgusted with either you or themselves. Connor, however, didn't budge from his spot. Instead, he reached out a hand to me. I blinked several times before I accepted it, too afraid of what he'd do if I didn't. He pulled me up to stand beside him.

"I'm sorry. I shouldn't have snapped like that."

His words surprised me. I think they surprised him as well.

"I don't usually let a pet into my living space," he continued, "nor do I attempt to train them this fast. You're bound to overstep. You don't know the rules yet." He shook his head once. "That's on me. But that doesn't make my warning any less true."

"What are the rules? Teach me, and I'll obey them—I don't wish to anger you," I tried.

"At this point, my rules won't matter—you'll only be with me through Saturday, then your new master will have a new set of instructions for you. It'll only confuse you to impart mine. For now, do as I say, when I say it. Don't try to escape or be a hero. It won't end well for you if you try. You believe me when I tell you that, don't you?"

I nodded. "I do."

His golden eyebrows pinched together. "I know I sound like a broken record, but it is imperative that you impress Malcolm." He took a deep breath, then went back to his desk. I stood where he left me, awaiting his instruction to move. I needed to gain his trust back, to move slower, even with such limited time. I'd gotten some information about Malcolm, but that it'd been more about the type of details Connor was looking for in a buyer. There wasn't anything technically illegal about background searches. I needed more—and to get that, Connor would need to trust me.

"Do you have anything I might use to strike up a conversation with him? Any special interests or hobbies I can pretend to know about?" I asked.

"There isn't much information on him." Connor frowned, peering at the screen. "He was born in Maine. His parents were poor, but later inherited a large sum of money from a deceased uncle, which he invested well. Moved to New York after graduation, and—"

"Where in Maine?"

He looked up at me. "Mid-coast. Why?"

"I grew up in that area," I said, "before I ran away. What town?"

Cocking his head, he turned back to his files. After clicking a few things, he leaned in to read one of the documents. "Um, looks like Swanville. Do you know it?"

I nodded. "I lived in East Belfast. Swanville's the next town over. You said he was turning thirty-two? I probably went to school with him, though I don't remember a Malcolm Luxx. Then again, I'm not great with names. But yeah, we may have gone to school together at some point. Waldo County isn't a big place."

"No shit?" Connor clapped his hands together. "That's it. Our in." He started typing frantically. "I never would've pegged you as a Maine girl."

"It wasn't too bad. Winters were brutal, but the summers were nice."

Connor offered a dismissive frown. "I'm no fan of the rain we get here, but snow in the amounts they get? Hard pass."

I shrugged. "I always loved the first snowstorm. The rust-colored world of dead leaves clinging to the branches would be covered in a matter of minutes in a blanket of white—all the ugly transformed into a clean slate. It's kind of magical. I used to think that maybe one day I could transform into something that beautiful too."

He looked at me a moment, seeming to take in what I'd said. "Perhaps Malcolm will be your blanket of snow."

"Perhaps," I agreed, but I didn't believe it. My life was perpetual decay and struggle. No one man would change that.

Connor went back to his screen, pulling up files until he seemed to find what he was searching for. "There!" He pointed to a photo from what looked like a yearbook. "Do you recognize him?"

I took a few steps closer to the screen to look at the black-and-white photo. A set of dark eyes with no smile looked back at me. Eyes I would remember until the day I died.

"Dayton Littlefield?" I gasped. I *did* know the guy—and had had the biggest crush on him.

"Dayton?" Connor scoffed. "Like Dayton, Ohio? No wonder he changed his name. Malcolm Luxx, you bastard—you have an alias too. No wonder it's been so hard to find dirt on you."

Leaning closer to the picture, I smiled. Somewhere in the world, there lived a yearbook of mine with a heart around this very picture. "He was my secret crush in high school, but he never once looked my way—though, to be fair, he didn't look anyone's way. He was a bit of a loner."

"With a name like that, can you blame him?" he replied. "Wow, what a small world. What are the odds that you two went to the same school? You have to marvel at it."

Dayton Littlefield. How crazy. I knew he'd get out of that tiny town and make something of himself. Dayton had been smarter than anyone at that school. He'd been beautiful, too, but hadn't seemed to know it—had always had his shoulders hunched, as though he was embarrassed by being so tall. How desperately I'd longed for his icy blue eyes to meet my gaze, just once.

"This is perfect," Connor said, rubbed his hands together. "This is the card we'll play on Saturday. It'll be my birthday gift to him—an introduction of a long-lost pal."

"We weren't actually pals," I interjected. "He didn't know I existed."

"Late-bloomer, were you?" he deadpanned.

"No, I got these in middle school." I nodded down at my chest.

"Then he knew you existed, trust me. He probably jacked off to the thought of those tits sliding up and down his cock on the regular."

Suddenly, he pushed up from the chair and lifted me off my feet, spinning me around. "Hot damn, I finally have a viable in with Malcolm Luxx—a *genuine* link to his past. Once he's seen how well you've grown into your body, he'll be more than ready to pay my finder's fee."

Holy shit. Would Malcolm be a way out for me? If he recognized me, he might pay Connor's fee...and then, someone with his wealth could figure out a way to save the girls. A new hand was being dealt, and I had to play it right.

CONNOR

After all this time, I was finally going to get Malcolm right where I wanted him. Amanda was learning quickly. She had a strong desire to live, and it would help her obey. Now, all I needed to do was ensure that their reunion would spark the fires I needed it to.

I grabbed Amanda by the arm and brought her into the kitchen. "Sit," I said, pointing at the table. Attached to the table was a large metal hoop with a pair of cuffs on it. "Lock yourself in."

Amanda looked at me, then at the cuffs, but quickly did as ordered.

"Stay," I said.

Walking back into the pet closet, I went to a box on the top shelf and pulled it down. Inside was an assortment of pill bottles. I lifted a few out, checking the labels, until I found the one I wanted. I shook one of the pills out and put the box away. Heading back into the kitchen, I filled a glass with water and brought it to her.

"Take this." I put the glass and the pill beside Amanda's free hand.

"What is it?"

I glared at her.

"Right. I'm not supposed to question your authority. It's just, I'm allergic to Ibuprofen—it gives me pretty nasty hives, and I'm assuming you don't want that for our meet and greet with Malcolm."

"It's Plan B."

She looked at the pill again. "Oh," she whispered.

"My pets are all on the pill, plus I wear a condom—neither of which we used earlier. I'm not risking bringing a spawn of mine into the world. One of me is bad enough, don't you think?"

I watched Amanda's expression carefully. She almost appeared to be struggling to take the pill. She wouldn't seriously want a child with me, would she? She couldn't be that insane.

"Children aren't born bad," she said at last. "They learn the behavior, usually from someone they love."

"Agreed. I learned my toxic traits from my mother." I laughed. "At least I feed you."

"How often did she withhold food from you?"

I clenched my jaw. I didn't want her pity. "Only when I disobeyed. It became a game we'd play: how long would she let me go without food?"

"What was your longest stretch?"

"Six days and five hours," I said without batting an eye. Amanda's eyes widened in horror, as they should. It had been utter hell. "A person can only last about a week without food and water," I continued, "did you know that? It's the lack of water that kills you, though. If you have water, you can last two, even three months. Mother knew that, which is why she refused me both." I laughed at the memory. "She always got me to comply, though."

"That's awful," she gasped.

"It was beyond torture—which is why I always make sure my pets are fed. Never forget I could be so much worse. Now, take the pill."

She picked up the pill and held it in her hands, before swallowing it down dry.

I ran my hand through my hair. "I'm going to go do some work. Sit and be a good girl. I'll come back for you soon."

Amanda nodded. Her eyes darted to the glass of water, but I quickly swiped it away. I wasn't about to leave something she could shatter and create a weapon with.

"I wasn't going to do anything with it," she said.

"Yeah, well, I'll rest easier knowing you can't."

I downed the water in front of her and took the glass with me back to my office. Time was short before tomorrow's meet and greet, and I needed to be ready. If Malcolm didn't take Amanda, I would need to prep her for the drive to Vincent. This adoption couldn't happen soon enough. I was getting far too used to having her around.

CHAPTER EIGHTEEN

AMANDA

Connor left me chained to the table for two hours—I knew because I watched the clock in the kitchen tick away the seconds. My bladder was in desperate need of relief, but I didn't want to bother him. I crossed my legs as tight as I could and bit my lip against the discomfort. A moment later, I heard the sound of a chair pushing out. Connor came out into the living room and stood in front of me.

"You are allowed to ask to use the restroom, you know."

I tilted my head, confused. I'd been so quiet. He looked behind him to the camera pointed at me. *Ah.* He'd been watching me. Of course he had.

"I didn't want to disturb your work."

"And I don't have the luxury of you getting a bladder infection. Come on." He leaned down and unlocked me, but kept a firm grip on my wrist as he led me toward the bathroom.

"Thank you," I said, expecting him to drop my hand so that I could use the restroom on my own. He didn't. Instead, Connor held onto my hand and guided me to the toilet—clearly, I wasn't to be trusted even to pee. Without any other choice, I pulled down the oversized sweats, sat down on the toilet, and peed with him watching my every move.

When I was finished, I had to wipe with my left hand, which was awkward. Then, Connor led me over to the sink, and I wondered if he'd let me wash my hands or not. I stood in front of the sink, and could see him contemplating in the mirror if he would release my hand. After a moment, he let my hand go, but stood behind me, pulling his arms around my waist to force our bodies together. The movement was so fast that I gasped. His hands dug into my hips, and I felt him grow hard behind me.

It was clear from his eyes that he wanted to take me. I wasn't stupid enough to resist him. It would be far smarter for me to play into his desires so I could take advantage of them later. Connor wasn't one to trust, so perhaps this was the best way to earn it: be as willing as possible.

To let him know I was ready, I leaned over the sink, lifting my ass in the air. I looked into the mirror to gauge his reaction. It was guarded, yet he didn't seem opposed to the idea.

My heart hammered in my chest, unsure if this would be something that pleased him or annoyed him. Connor ran hot and cold, so that I never knew where I stood with him...which is probably how he wanted it.

"Give me your hands," he said.

For a moment, I wondered if that meant he wanted me to stand up, but I risked putting my hands behind my back. The second I did, he grabbed my wrists easily with one hand, and with the other, yanked the sweatpants down to my knees. A moment later, he slid two fingers inside of me. I let out a moan of shock.

"Well, that's interesting," he murmured.

"What is?"

Connor moved expertly in and out of my folds. Unable to resist, I panted along with his movements. He was shockingly good at this.

"How wet you are for me," he responded. "The others are always so dry. I have to lube them. But you..." He removed his fingers, and I felt their loss instantly. "You have consistently been ready for me."

Watching me in the mirror, he took off his shirt and then pulled down his pants with his free hand. The sound of the fabric dropping to the floor sent an unexpected thrill through me. His cock was hard. His hand touched my ass, and I felt my mouth water in anticipation.

"Do you know what that wetness means, Amanda?"

A moment later, Connor pushed himself inside me, filling me instantly. I cried in unexpected delight. He lowered himself against my back. Hot in my ear he whispered, "It means I turn you on."

"Yes," I panted. "God, yes." And it was true. As twisted and sadistic as it was, there was something about this man that aroused me beyond all sense or reason. I ached for him to fuck me, as I'd never ached for a man before. It was terribly confusing to think such things of your captor. But with Connor's thighs slapping against my ass, there was little thinking to be done—just desire and need. Terrible, terrible need.

"Amanda, I want you to listen to me very carefully," he said, pushing himself back up to stand. My legs spread wide as he slowed his thrusts.

"I'm listening."

"You are not allowed to come. Do you understand?" he purred. "I am going to finish, but you must not come. If you do, I will punish you—and I promise you, you will not like it. But if you obey, you'll be rewarded. Understood?"

I nodded, but I wasn't sure I could stop myself. I was already so close. As if he knew what type of torture this was, Connor pushed himself inside me slowly, digging the fingers of his left hand hard into my hips.

Each thrust inside me was slow and deliberate. I pinched my eyes closed, trying to think of anything to cool my libido—doing the dishes, shoveling, Nicholas Cage's stupid wig in Con Air—anything to take my mind off being so aroused.

"Open your eyes, Amanda. I want to see your eyes when I come."

Whimpering, I forced my eyes onto the mirror where they

locked with his. My lips dropped open in longing, and Connor slapped my ass, hard. I let out a yelp of pleasure.

"I said 'no.'" His gaze was a warning, and I bit back my desire, focusing instead on the pain stinging my ass. I tried hard to concentrate on the pain and not the bizarre desire it brought. I had to obey his order, but I wanted to come so badly.

Our bodies slapped together in a wild frenzy and at about the moment I was about to come undone, punishment be damned, Connor groaned and shuddered inside of me. He kept his thighs pressed against mine for a few moments as his breathing steadied, and I took that opportunity to regulate my own heart. This was *not* the way I had seen this trip to the bathroom going.

"Did you come?" he asked.

I shook my head vehemently.

"Good girl," he said. "You can get your reward then. Stand up and take the hoodie off."

All too willingly, I did as he asked. I *wanted* him to reward me. As I stood before him, naked, nipples erect for his gaze, there was no denying the signals my body was giving me—I was very, very turned on. By my fucking captor.

What the hell was wrong with me?

CONNOR

As Amanda stood in front of me, my eyes fell instantly on her perfect breasts, longing to suck and tug them with my teeth. Shaking my head, I focused on something safer: her full lips. They were parted as her chest rose and fell, but not with fear.

She was horny as fuck. For me.

It was so strange to see her look at me like this. All my other captives put up a good face, but there was always an edge of fear in their eyes. Pain. Disgust. Never had one of the pets been so ready for me to enter them, so full of need. Sure, it was plausible that

Amanda was a very good actress, giving me what she thought I wanted, but women couldn't fake being wet—that wasn't something a person could do. It had to be triggered by a physical response. It was clear that Amanda desired me...and it was hot as hell.

She'd done well to hold off her orgasm—it meant that she wanted to please me more than she wanted to please herself, that my need was more important than her own. That's what any good pet should think, but it was hardly ever the reality. A pet's needs were inconsequential to a master. Once I sold Amanda off to Malcolm, I would no longer be in control of her. It was only out of kindness that I wanted to make sure she had one memorable night of being fucked properly by a master.

"Hold out your hands."

She quickly put them in front of her. From the drawer by the sink, I pulled out a set of plastic ties. Making quick work out of them, I secured her hands together and guided her to the shower.

"Get in," I said, watching her naked ass with my red handprint on it as she obeyed. I got in behind her and closed the shower door. Even though Amanda did as I ordered, I couldn't believe what I was doing. This was dangerous. *Foolish.* We didn't have time to waste on something like this, yet I was incapable of stopping. I wanted to taste her too badly.

"Lift your arms."

She swallowed, but did as she was told. Above her was a rope with a caliper attached. I slipped the caliper through her ties until she was standing in front of me, helpless to escape. Then, I removed her ankle monitor.

"I'm going to bathe you and shave you, get you all pretty for tomorrow. Then, if you're a good girl, I'm going to eat your pussy. Would you like that?"

Amanda's responding whimper and nod told me everything I needed to know. She was still very horny. I turned on the water, reaching for the razor and shaving cream.

"Now hold very, very still," I said, dancing the blade in front of her face. She bit her bottom lip, and it was all I could do not to take her again right here and now.

No, Connor. Focus. This shower is necessary for Malcolm's enjoyment, not yours. This is a job, damn it. You are preparing her to fuck another man.

"Let's begin," I said—unable to stop a grin from sliding across my lips.

CHAPTER NINETEEN

Amanda

As the water trickled down my naked body, I watched Connor's every movement. Sure, I could use my legs to kick him, but what good would that do? With my hands bound, I was helpless to escape. He could do anything he wanted to me, and I wouldn't be able to stop him. That alone was terrifying and titillating at the same time.

He twirled the razor blade handle in his fingers a few times, as if to warn me—one wrong move, and he'd have that blade at my neck. I didn't need the reminder. I knew full well who was in control of the situation. Once Connor appeared satisfied that I'd be compliant, he sank to his knees. I sucked in a breath, noticing how close his head was to my core. He seemed to give the area a longing look, before focusing on the task at hand: shaving my legs. Placing the razor on the shelf behind him, he grabbed a bar of soap. He brought the bar up my leg slowly, seductively, inching it up my thigh until it landed in my pubic hair. He rubbed the soap in slow circles as the bubbles built around the bar. The pressure mounting inside me grew with his proximity to my entrance.

"Don't worry. I know you women need to be careful what goes inside you" Carefully, he ran the bar along the outside of my folds, and I closed my eyes. "That's why I'll be licking that area clean once your legs are done."

I am ashamed to admit that I hoped that was a promise and not a threat, because hot damn, the way he was looking at me from down on his knees, the water tricking down his face...it made me ache for him to touch me. This was so, so wrong.

His attention went back to shaving my legs once I had been lathered appropriately. He was slow and careful around the knee, which told me that he'd done this before. *With his other pets*. Right. I had to remember that I was still very much his captive. There were other girls locked away in prisons of their own at this very moment. This was not the time to be fantasizing about getting oral. *Focus, Amanda!*

That's when I felt something hot on my upper thigh—his lips, sucking hard, so hard it stung.

"What are you doing?" I asked, then pinched my lips shut, scolding myself.

Instead of being angry, Connor stopped his assault, pulling his lips off me. The area below them was all red. "Malcolm may be able to lay claim to you tomorrow," he said, "but I want him to know I tasted you first."

That shouldn't be hot—right?

"And now, Amanda, for your reward."

He spread my legs apart and I didn't put up any struggle. "God, yes," I breathed, my words offering him permission. Not that he required it.

"You naughty girl," he said, sliding a finger inside of me. I closed my eyes in delight. "You're still so wet."

"You make me that way," I said honestly.

Connor's hands gripped my hips hard to hold me in place—not that I was going to fight him off, not when I was so hungry with need. He kept his finger inside of me, pulling it in and out, studying my reaction, watching for the moment when he found my clit. My mouth fell open as he pressed against the delicate flesh. Smiling, he removed his finger and replaced it with his tongue.

I couldn't help it—I screamed out in pleasure. Connor's tongue was like magic as it circled and pressed in just the right spot. I longed to dig my fingers into his hair, to pull him closer to me, but my bindings didn't allow it. I did the only thing I could do which was to lift my hips to give him more of me. Round and round my clit he explored me, sucking and circling, teasing me to the edge of my control.

"Fuck, Connor! Right there," I screamed, knowing full well I should have kept my mouth shut. "Please," I begged, "may I come?"

He removed his tongue from me, granting his permission with a nod. Then, he returned his magical tongue to me and pressed against me, causing me to let out a groan of ecstasy. Unable to resist, I shattered against his tongue, my entire body shaking with my orgasm. Before Connor pulled his tongue from my folds, I could've sworn I felt him smile.

"Holy fuck," I gasped.

Connor stood up and grabbed me by the back of the head, holding me in place. "You came for me," he murmured. "Now, it's time you experience what a good girl tastes like." A second later, his tongue, the same one that had been between my thighs seconds before, was now inside my mouth. Instead of being disgusted, it turned me on even more.

My tongue danced against his, my body desperately trying to get closer to him without the use of my arms. With only one leg to use, I hitched my right one over Connor's hip, pulling him closer to me, which earned me a hard slap on the ass—but holy hell, that only made me want to do it again.

"So naughty," he whispered hotly against my ear, as my lips parted in desire. "I'm going to miss fucking you. Malcolm better snatch you up, or I might be tempted to keep you for myself."

If I got sold off, any chance of saving the other girls would likely be over—and, depending on who I was sold off to, my life might be over as well. As crazy as it was, staying with the devil I knew was the smartest play. Connor just couldn't know that it was a play.

"What's going on inside that pretty head of yours?" Connor took a step back, pulling away from me. "I can tell you're thinking about something. Tell me."

"It's just...would that be so terrible? Keeping me all to yourself?"

Any trace of humanity drained out of his face. I had said the wrong thing. He turned off the water, glaring at me as he did.

"As punishment for that question, you will stand there and air dry."

"But—" The second I spoke, I knew I'd been wrong. When Connor's hand raised a second later, I closed my eyes and braced for the smack. I'd been hit plenty of times by dirtbags growing up. I could take it. The slap, however, did not come to my face, but instead landed on my breast. Instantly, a red mark appeared—a mark that would be hidden from view. I bit my tongue to hide the pain.

"You do not want to be mine," Connor growled. "I would not be kind to you. Never forget that I am a monster, Amanda. *Never.*"

With that, he left me shivering at his retreat. My options were looking grimmer and grimmer by the moment.

CONNOR

I was fuming. I'd lost my cool with her, and that was a huge mistake—it let the pets know they'd gotten to me. But even hinting that Amanda could stay with me? Impossible. It had shaken me in a way I hadn't anticipated. This wasn't the first time a pet had asked me to keep them—far from it. It often came as part of the bargaining phase of their captivity, when they were still coming to terms with their situation. But with the others, I'd seen it for what it was—something motivated by their fear of what was yet to come for them, fighting to stay in the hell they knew. But with Amanda...I think she legitimately meant it, that she actually wanted to be with *me*. Which was both insane and idiotic if true.

No, it couldn't be. It was an act. She didn't have feelings for me. She was a desperate woman, clinging to hope.

Then why is she always so wet for you?

Shaking my head, I grabbed both towels from the bathroom, wrapped one around my waist, and tossed the other on my bed. Maybe shivering alone in the shower would make her realize I wasn't going to be kind to her. She wasn't special. She didn't mean anything to me. She was merchandise—*merchandise I had felt compelled to leave my mark on.*

I cursed. I shouldn't have done that. Men were very territorial. If Malcolm did buy Amanda tomorrow and take her to bed, he'd see the places I'd marked her, and it would be clear that she'd been recently soiled. He might want to renege on the whole deal...I might have already blown it.

"Chill, Connor. He hasn't even said he'd buy her yet. One step at a time."

Still, the image of that hickey on Amanda's inner thigh burned behind my eyelids. Why was she so much fun to fuck? I mean, I always got off when screwing a pet, a hole was a hole, but with her...it was next-level. Even though I'd just had her, I found myself wondering if I'd be able to take her again before tomorrow. The thought of entering her wet pussy made my cock swell.

"Fuck," I hissed down at my dick. I was hard again.

Damn this woman.

Without thinking, I spun on my heel and went back into the bathroom. There she was, shivering, her head low. Compliant. Waiting for instructions. Like a good girl.

I opened the shower door and removed her from the hook. "Get out." My words were firm, and she obeyed them quickly. "Go to my bed. Lay down on the towel, face-up."

Amanda's eyes met mine briefly as she walked into my room. She crawled onto the bed as best she could with tied hands, making sure to show her ass to me as she made her way to the towel. Once there, she laid on her back, placed her arms above her head, and looked over at me, awaiting my next command. I went over to where I'd dropped my pants and fished out my knife, cutting off the plastic ties around her wrists.

"If you make me regret taking these off, I'll cuff all your limbs. Understood?"

She nodded, those big blue eyes gazing at me with undeniable hunger. *Fuck.*

"Spread your legs" I ordered.

I swear her eyes lit up as she obeyed, eagerly opening her slit wide for me. *Damn her to hell.*

Removing my towel, I dropped it to the ground and climbed onto the bed, saddling her between my thighs. Her breath hitched as her back arched, presenting her breasts up to me like a goddamn gift. They were too perfect to ignore. My lips latched onto one as I guided my dick inside her. *Still wet for me.*

Her hands dug into the sheets, and I could tell she wanted to use that energy on me instead.

"You may touch me," I said, coming up from her nipple before I moved over to the other. She moaned her delight and instantly put her hands on my back, pulling me closer to her. Every fiber in my being wanted to claim her as mine. If I didn't know better, I could've sworn she wanted the same.

"God, you feel so good," she panted against my ear. The words pulled my focus to her lips, where I wanted so desperately to kiss her, but I resisted. She might see how much I wanted her if I let her kiss me again—far safer to keep this to strict fucking.

When her hands merged down to my ass, I lost all thought, her touch triggering my climax. I froze inside of her as I let myself pour into of her. She clung to me like a lifejacket, with feverish fingers that didn't seem to want to let me go. Finally, I collapsed on top of her, winded—the most spent I'd ever felt after fucking a pet.

This woman held some sort of power over me...which made her extremely dangerous.

Rolling off her, I stood up and cleaned myself off with the towel at my feet. Walking over to her side of the bed, I pulled out the draw of the nightstand and withdrew a leather cord with a cuff at the end.

"Give me your foot."

Amanda looked at me, then at the strap, but presented me with her foot. I placed it on my chest as I secured the cuff around her ankle. The other end I secured to the lock at the foot of my bed. While I'd never allowed a pet to sleep in my bed before, I always kept toys inside my nightstand for any other guest I might entertain.

"Go to sleep," I said, putting her foot down and pulling the covers over her naked body. "You need to be rested for Malcolm tomorrow."

I saw the look in her eyes as I said Malcolm's name. She was disappointed; she didn't want to leave me. Well, that was too fucking bad. I was not about to let this woman into my life—not today, not ever. My world held no place for such luxuries. That was the last time I'd fuck her.

I needed her gone.

CHAPTER TWENTY

Amanda

Connor left me chained to his bed, naked, while he went back to his computer to work on my file for Malcolm.

My mind and emotions were reeling. On the one hand, I'd consistently had the best sex of my life with Connor—but on the other, he *was* the man who'd kidnapped me, a man that would never be cured of his demons. There would never come a day when he'd reach redemption for the hell he'd put all these women through. Even so, there was a small part of me that saw the broken child within him, how his past had shaped his future. I felt sorry for the suffering Connor must have endured to become this way... and I realized that sympathy made me a monster too.

When I awoke the next morning, it was to the feeling of Connor's arms wrapped tightly around me. He must have slept in the bed with me. His arms caged us together, wrapped around my stomach, holding me close to him as lovers do. It was odd seeing him sleep like this, so quiet and vulnerable, though he still didn't look peaceful. Behind his lids, I could see his eyes moving frantically, deep in REM sleep.

As I watched him sleep, the gentle curve of his lips went from slack to troubled. The lines between his brows deepened as his breathing picked up. His mouth twitched.

"No," he mumbled in his sleep. I froze, not wanting to wake him. "Leave her alone, Mother!" His arms pulled me closer to his chest, nearly crushing me. "She's mine. I won't let you hurt her too. Stop!"

At that, Connor's eyes ripped open. He looked down at me, with his hands still laced around my body, and instantly retreated. He got out of bed, and in the same motion, ripped the sheets off me. My eyes drank in his nakedness. He seemed to be orienting himself to the fact that I was in his bed, that he'd been holding me. That's when I noticed his cock growing erect. The anger in his eyes turned hungry, and I was ashamed to admit that I dampened on the spot.

"Roll over. Get on your hands and knees," Connor commanded, eyes locked onto mine. It sent a shiver of desire through me, and I rolled over as he requested.

Feeling his hand cup my ass, I let out a soft moan of anticipation, before the sharp sting of his slap caused my knees to buckle. With my face buried in the sheets, I felt his hands grip my waist and bring me back to kneeling.

"My handprint was fading," he said calmly.

I didn't say anything. I knew he would be angry if I did. My place was to be ready for whatever he wanted to do to me, but here was the kicker—I *wanted* him to hit my ass again. The sting was still radiating on my cheek, and my other one was jealous.

I *wanted* him to hit me. How fucked up was that?

For a moment, Connor didn't say anything. I longed to turn my head to see if he was even still in the room, but before I could, I felt his fingers enter me. I gasped.

"You're wet." He seemed surprised. "Amanda, when I slapped your ass just now, did that turn you on?"

He asked a direct question, so I knew I would be allowed to speak. I decided to be as honest as I could. "You always make me wet. It doesn't matter what it is that you do to me. It's you. You *do* things to me, even though I know you shouldn't, even though I *know* I should be repulsed by you. I'm just...not. I want you, even now."

"You want me?" he repeated.

"I do." I risked a glance behind me to see him looking at me. His head cocked to the side.

"Don't move."

Swallowing down my desire, I nodded and waited for him on hands and knees, aching for him to screw me. Listening intently, I heard him walk across the room to retrieve something. A moment later, my foot was released from its prison.

"Lay in the center of the bed," Connor commanded. "On your back." Complying willingly, I turned over and did as he instructed. "Hands over your head. Legs apart."

He would get no arguments from me. My whole body was a live wire, aching to feel his hands on mine. Slowly, Connor climbed up onto the bed, his knees straddling either side of my hips. All he'd need to do is reach down and guide himself into my eagerly awaiting core. I bit back my lust, waiting for him to ravish me.

CONNOR

Amanda lay beneath me, ready and waiting. Her sudden wetness at my touch couldn't be explained away by anything other than desire. She wanted me. *Me.* The very one hurting her. It didn't make any sense—nor did it make sense that I was allowing her to be unchained again on my bed. She couldn't get far if she tried to run, but looking at her now, with her eyes staring back at me...I *knew* she wasn't going to. Escape wasn't on her mind. What she wanted was me inside of her.

The opportunity was too tempting to ignore: one last fuck to get her out of my head. If this was to be our last time together, I wanted to make sure I remembered it. So I took a big gamble and leaned down—kissing her hard, full on the lips.

When Amanda's tongue brushed against mine, I grew even harder. She was kissing me back—not because she had to, but because she wanted to. It was intoxicating. My hands slid up her arms, locking her wrists in place. I could take her right here, fuck her brains out, keep her locked tight between my thighs...but then, a devilish impulse came over me, one I had never entertained with a pet before. Still, I found it irresistible. It was a move that might be my last, but I had to risk it. My cock demanded it.

In one fell swoop, I rolled my body over until Amanda was on top of me. A pet. *On top.* Unheard of. I had placed myself in the submissive position, had released my power to her. It was the most sexually-vulnerable I'd ever allowed myself to be with someone. What Amanda did with this power would determine if she lived or died.

Her eyes peered down at me, shocked as well that she was allowed to mount me. Her hair cascaded down her face, her breasts dangling before me like forbidden fruit. I wanted to suckle them again, but I also needed to know if Amanda would try and run, or if she would follow my command. She wasn't pinned down in any way, shape, or form. My body was no longer caging her. She could hurt me. In one move, she could reach down and try to tear off my cock, and I would be helpless to avoid the pain. But if she did that, she'd be signing her own death warrant—she wouldn't escape my room or this building alive.

I had placed the ball in her court—literally.

To challenge her even more, I raised my hands over my head, totally open to her. It was her move.

"Amanda," I said.

Her eyes were wide, as though realizing the shift in power herself. "Yes?"

"What are you thinking?"

She swallowed once, before licking her lips. "I'm thinking I'd very much like for you to be inside me."

An odd wave of relief and desire rocked through me. "So put my cock in your pussy, then."

Her eyes danced in delight. "Fuck, yes."

With permission granted, she reached her hand down and guided my dick inside her wetness, both moaning in desire as our bodies connected. She rocked against me, slowly at first, as if savoring the feeling. Her hands moved to her breasts as she increased her rhythm.

"Amanda," I said, surprised by the husky tone that escaped my lips. "Do you want me to touch you?"

She looked down at me with lustful eyes. "Please," she begged.

"What do you want me to do? Tell me. Be specific." I watched her eyes as she processed my request.

"Grab my hips."

I did as she commanded, and she smacked her body against mine.

"Fuck—*harder*, Connor. Hold onto me like you don't ever want to let me go," she panted. Her breasts bobbed up and down, sending me into a tizzy. Wanting to appease her, my fingers dug into the flesh of her hips, pulling her body closer to me with every downward motion. She threw her head back, letting me see her perfect breasts glistening with her sweat. Her right hand drifted down to her pussy, massaging her clit. Her eyes closed against the sensation, and the room filled with the sounds of skin slapping against skin.

"My breasts," she screamed. "Grab my breasts, now."

More than ready to comply, I moved my hands from her waist to cover each perfect breast. I rolled each nipple between my thumbs and she leaned her head back, moaning in a way that made my cock drive into her even harder. We were in perfect sync.

A second later, Amanda screamed out her release, shaking delicately around me. I was close, but needed a few more thrusts. Twisting her hips, I rolled her onto her back. Her lips parted in pure bliss as she lifted each of her legs to my shoulders.

"My turn," I growled.

Like a jackhammer, I pounded my dick into her slick core, again and again. Her eyes went cross-eyed as I fucked her as hard as I could. My own climax danced through my entire body, and I exploded inside her once again.

I collapsed on top of her, locking my arms around her—not to pin her down, but because I knew, in that moment, that I didn't want to let her go. *Ever.*

Fuck me. I was so screwed.

CHAPTER TWENTY-ONE

Amanda

This was bad. I was having feelings for my captor.

I was smart enough to know that it was a trauma response, at least—a self-defense mechanism to keep me from mentally snapping under the reality of my situation. I knew all about trauma response. I'd lived with an abuser for years, had grown up with mistreatment. It was all I knew.

The difference with Connor, however, was that I was physically attracted to him. It wasn't an act that I put on in hopes of getting a lesser beating—I *wanted* him to throw me down and have his way with me. I wanted his cock inside me, longed for the feel of his arms around me as they were now. *That* was the part I'd need a therapist to help me sort out...if I ever escaped this situation.

Without looking at me, Connor pulled himself out of me and sat on the edge of the bed. I longed to get up and curl my arms around his shoulders, but something about the way he sat there told me that if I did, it might be the last thing I'd ever do. Instead, I stayed put on the bed, waiting for his command.

"It's time to go." Connor's voice was clipped, cold.

He got out of bed and went to his closet, pulling on a pair of black boxer briefs, before taking out a silvery-gray pair of slacks.

"Your dress is here," he said, opening the door of the cabinet beside him. "Put it on."

Nodding, I stood up. His semen ran down my leg. I reached for a tissue to clean myself off, but he stopped me.

"No, leave it. I want Malcolm to know I was there first."

Swallowing, I walked over to the closet and took out a red dress. It was different from the one he'd shown me before—classy yet sexy. The swoop neck would give Malcolm a full view of my breasts, while the snug fit would allude to my other assets. There, on the hanger with the dress, was my bra: the same one Connor had taken from me the day I'd come to view the apartment.

"I told you I'd give it back," he said from behind me.

I'd wanted to reply, say something snarky or flirtatious, but I knew any response would be wrong. This was so complicated.

"Let me help you," Connor offered. He reached out, taking the bra from my hands. He turned my back to him, and held the bra in front of me. Slowly, I placed an arm in each hole. He fastened it on its tightest setting before he spun me around and frowned. "They need a little adjusting."

Connor's fingers slipped under my breasts and lifted both fully out of the cup, before leaning down and suckling each, hard. His teeth dragged over my nipples one last time before letting them fall. Sighing, he placed each breast back into its cup.

Once both my breasts were tucked safely away from his hungry lips, he spun me around slowly, handing me the dress.

"No panties," he said as he went back to dressing himself.

Nodding, I slid the dress over my head, and Connor paused putting on his tie to help me zip up the back. His head lowered to the nape of my neck, as I felt him inhale me. A moment later, those strong fingers dug into my hips, and he held me against him. We stood there for several minutes, not saying anything, just breathing each other in, holding each other, before Connor cleared his throat and told me to sit on the bed. I went willingly.

I sat and watched him finish getting dressed. When he

buttoned his jacket, I caught his reflection in the mirror. *Seriously sexy in a suit.* He looked at me and pointed one finger.

"Stay."

Like I could go anywhere. He knew this, but still, he gave the order.

When Connor came back into the room, he held the ankle monitor again. "Give me your foot and take this." He handed me another pill. Right—another Plan B. I swallowed it dry, then lifted my right leg so he could attach the monitor. "The boots will slip right over this. No one will know."

Nodding, I hunted for Connor's eyes, desperate for him to realize this was a mistake—that he didn't want to sell me off, that he wanted to keep me. If he kept me, I knew I'd find a way to save the others. Connor needed someone to love him, to care about him. It was obvious to me that he'd never been shown any true love in his life. I could do that for him. Then, he'd finally be able to see how much hurt he was causing. I'd be able to help him *and* the other women—I was sure of it.

"Lie down," he said once the monitor was secure. For half a second, I thought he was going to take me again. "I need to feed the other pets before we go. The roofie you took will kick in soon. When you wake, we'll be well on our way to Malcolm's party."

At that, my eyes grew wide. *Roofie?*

"What—you didn't think I'd let you know where a client lives, did you? Don't fight the sleep, it'll just give you a headache."

"You drugged me?" I heard myself whisper.

"Monster, remember? Now, lay back down before *I* lay you down." He took a step toward me, hand ready to fly—a move I knew all too well.

I did as he commanded and laid down, waiting for the drugs to pull me under.

CONNOR

Once Amanda had passed out, I secured her to the bed. It was unlikely that she'd wake up, but on the off chance she'd faked her sleep, I had to protect myself. In the kitchen, I pulled out the brown paper bags I'd prepped for lunches a few days ago, going with a nostalgic PB and J, carrot sticks, and a protein bar. There were no wrappers or baggies, but even so, the pets would eat like queens today. Gathering the bags in one arm, I secured my unit and went down the row of cages.

At each pet's door, I dumped the contents of their food on the floor. They had long lost the desire to eat like civilized creatures. It was all part of the training. Once they left here, they'd know how good they had it, and wouldn't ever complain—the threat of being sent back to me for misbehaving would be too great.

As I was finishing up the last delivery, the elevator dinged. The doors slid open, and Kenny came out. His hair was slicked back, and he was wearing a white suit with a dark blue shirt and tie. One of my old ones. He was too short for it, and the legs pooled at the feet.

"Your limo awaits." Kenny smiled. "She ready for transport?" He nodded toward Amanda's room.

"Thanks, Kenny, but your services aren't needed tonight after all. I'm going to drive her to the location myself."

Kenny raised an eyebrow. I had never done such a thing. I would have questioned myself too.

"Timid client," I explained. "He's going to need different tactics."

He nodded. "Sure, sure. At least let me get her in the car for you." Kenny made a move toward Amanda's room. Even though she wasn't her normal cage, I stopped him by grabbing a fistful of his jacket.

"You are not to lay a finger on her. Understood?"

Kenny took a step back, eyes showing a sudden panic. "Yes, sir."

I let him go. "This is an extremely important adoption. Nothing can go wrong. I need to handle it myself. Are we clear?"

"Crystal."

"Follow in a car behind me. Be my eyes. Watch her like a hawk."

"Is she a flight risk?"

I felt myself shaking my head. "No, and that's what concerns me. If she makes any attempt to leave my side until I sell her, I'm going to offload her on Vincent."

Kenny nodded once, his hand inadvertently resting on his hidden piece. A moment later, he headed back to the elevator, and I went back to gather Amanda—one last chance to hold her in my arms, before I sold her to be used for another man's pleasure.

Back in my bedroom, I stood over Amanda's lifeless body. Sitting down beside her, I ran my fingers delicately over her arm. Was this something I could ever have? A woman in my bed who wanted to be there? It had seemed impossible before Amanda walked into my life. Fighting every urge to call Malcolm and tell him we wouldn't be attending his party after all, I undid her restraint and scooped her up in my arms. Her head landed against my neck, and the feel of her hot breath against my skin had me pulling her closer.

"Please, Malcolm," I whispered. "Take her off my hands, so I don't make the stupidest decision of my life and keep her."

CHAPTER TWENTY-TWO

MALCOLM

Three hours and twenty-two minutes: that was how much longer I had to endure this yearly proof of life ritual. I loathed being in public like this. It was a threat not only to my safety, as I had many enemies, but it was also a big fat lie. I didn't live in this house. I owned it, sure, but it wasn't where I called home. This mansion was a ruse to make clients think I had a permanent residence—I'd even hired men who looked like me to live in the house now and then, in case I was being watched. Paranoid? Perhaps, but it'd kept my alibis secure when I had been otherwise occupied, doing things the law would rather I didn't. No one needed to know that I was mobile nearly all the time. Being anywhere for longer than a week made me twitchy.

If it wasn't for the fact that I met most of my yearly clients at this one party, I would stop throwing them altogether. Despite my reclusive nature, everyone was clamoring to get a painting by the famous Malcolm Luxx. Little did they know, I didn't paint most of them. I stole them from lesser-known and far more talented artists than myself.

Well, "stole" was a strong word. The artists I procured pieces from were compensated for their art, just in an indirect way. They'd wake to find a piece missing, but a few weeks later, a large windfall would come their way. I paid them for their work—more than what they were worth, to be sure—but I oversold them for at least five times what I paid. I wasn't evil, I just couldn't keep up with the demand. I'd found a way of cheating the system, and as long as I kept my alibis strong, no one could accuse me of stealing. It was a perfect scheme.

Shaking the hand of yet another person whose name I wouldn't remember, I looked over at one of my assistants, Darcy, who gave me a nod. She'd see that they'd get my contact information. She was one of the very few I let into my private little world—well, she and her wife, Camila. They ran the administrative end of things. I trusted them completely.

Beside me, Camila handed me a glass of champagne. "You told me to let you know when Connor Brooks arrived," she smiled, faking a wave to someone across the room. "Well, the security cameras indicate he's pulled up now, with a plus one. A redhead. Your favorite." Camila smirked as she looked over to the door, awaiting their arrival.

"I don't have favorites," I said, taking the glass and downing a large swig. "I'm going to duck out for a few. Cover for me, would you? Reiterate to Mr. Brooks that I'm not interested."

"You don't even want to look at her? She was stunning on the monitor."

I turned to look at Camila. "No, I do not. I have no desire to have any dealings with that man. You're aware of what it is he sells, aren't you?"

"Escorts aren't as taboo as they used to be," she said.

Lowering my voice, I locked eyes with her. "No, he doesn't sell escorts—he sells sex slaves And not just for a night. He sells them outright. He's selling *human beings*."

At that, Camila's dark eyes widened. "No shit?" Her face blanched. "Why haven't you reported him?"

"Because my own record is so squeaky clean? Those who live in glass houses..." I trailed off. "Besides, Brooks is a very powerful man, with a lot of dark connections. Not the sort of person you want on your shit list."

"*Pfft*. Good luck finding you...well, outside of tonight, that is."

"Just do me a favor—get rid of him. I'm guessing he'll give up if he doesn't run into me, but in case he lingers for more than half an hour, see him to the door."

"Can do." She gave me a firm nod, and I retreated into my study to watch the action from the screens inside. Each room of the house could be monitored from my study. It was my safe room. Every location I stayed at had such a place. I trusted no one, especially men like Connor. Connor was about as dangerous as they came in the underworld. His *thugs* had thugs. He was at the top of a dark and twisted food chain. Even dismissing him at my own party was a risky move, but one I had to make. I wanted no associations with him, or the women he was peddling.

Pouring myself a bourbon, I sat down in one of the leather chairs closest to the monitors—I wanted to witness the moment Connor Brooks' hope of pawning off one of his "pets" on me left his eyes. The man was vile for what he did, and while several of my clients had pets of their own, it was not something I could abide by. Stealing and then paying for art anonymously was not akin to selling *people*.

I focused my attention on the front door monitor as they approached. Connor was blocking the woman from view as he was let into the house. His solid frame stepped inside, still hiding his "present" for me. I wondered if she even knew why she was here, and shook my head. Connor was wasting his time with me. No matter how many adoption papers he sent my way, I wouldn't bite. Even if I was into that level of kink, which I wasn't, there was no way I'd put myself in that position. The second I bought anything from that man, he would have leverage over me, and could threaten to expose what I'd done if I didn't comply with his demands. I wasn't about to be put under anyone's thumb.

I thought I'd made that clear after the last dozen disposals of his "adoption" papers. Yet still, he persisted. The fool thought he hadn't found my type yet, but that was just it—I didn't *have* a type. Not anymore. I'd turned that part of me off a long time ago. There had only ever been one woman who had my heart, and she didn't even know my name.

That's when Connor stepped further into the house, and I got to see the woman he'd brought for me for the first time. Blinking, I nearly dropped my drink.

It was *her*. Amanda Jackson. My secret high school obsession. I would recognize those lush lips anywhere. And those eyes—how I'd longed for her to look my way even once. Not a soul knew this, but I still carried her yearbook picture in my wallet.

What was she doing with that scum?

One look at the way Connor's fingers dug deep into her waist told me everything I needed to know about his "business," confirming what I believed to be true, but didn't want to look too closely at. These women were not sex slaves willingly. They were forced into this life.

"Fuck." Putting down my bourbon, I paced the study. There was no way Connor could have known about my feelings for Amanda—I'd never told a soul about her. Was it dumb luck, then, that the only woman I'd ever loved had miraculously walked into my house on my birthday, in Connor Brooks' clutches? I wasn't one for believing in a higher power, but it did feel like this was divine intervention. Amanda needed help, and I was possibly the only person on the planet equipped to handle a guy like Connor. One thing was clear: I couldn't let him leave with her. He'd sell her off to the next bidder.

So what? She isn't your problem.

I glanced back at the screen and focused on Amanda. While her smile was plastered on, her eyes were searching for help—for someone, anyone, to unchain her from her fate.

Digging out my cell, I texted Darcy.

Bring Mr. Brooks and his guest to the study.

A moment passed before she replied.

> I'm sorry, did you say you wanted to see Mr. Brooks?

Yes.

> Redheads. I knew it. I'm weak for them too.

I shoved my phone back into my pocket and began to pace again. What was I going to say to him? Would Amanda recognize me? No, she wouldn't—I was a nobody back then. I hadn't had my growth spurt yet, and had been about twenty pounds heavier. Still, I needed to help her. No one deserved to live under his thumb, and knowing Brooks, the second he caught a whiff of the fact that I wanted her, he'd up his price. Not that the price would matter. I didn't want his business in any way connected to mine.

I needed to find a way to play this cool—and soon—before he showed up in my study.

CONNOR

"Keep that smile on, Amanda," I whispered in her ear. "One of his assistants is coming our way, either to kick us out, or invite us in for a conversation. By now, Malcolm should have had a good look at you— and you'd better hope, for your sake, that you impressed." I turned on my killer charm as the petite woman with a dark pixie cut approached.

"Mr. Brooks, I'm Darcy, Mr. Luxx's executive assistant."

I reached out and took her proffered hand, bringing it up to my lips to kiss. The look in her eyes told me I was barking up the wrong tree. I needed to try a different tactic.

"Lovely party," I began. "I can only assume you're the one who threw together this affair?"

"Flattery will get you everywhere, Mr. Brooks." She gave me a small smile before glancing at Amanda. I didn't miss the once-over that she'd made of Amanda's physique. A slight twitch of her lips confirmed my hunch: she'd rather have Amanda's attention than mine. "Mr. Luxx has asked to speak with the two of you privately, if you have a moment?" Her eyes came back to me, and I did my best not to show my excitement.

"We'd be honored. Lead the way."

Darcy gave me a slight nod, then turned to walk us through the living room, past the kitchen, and to an area that looked to be a small study. There was no one inside.

"Mr. Luxx will be with you in a moment."

"Thank you, Darcy."

Once she was gone, I took Amanda's shoulders and gave them a slight squeeze. "Speak only if I permit you. Do you understand?"

Amanda nodded once. Just then, the bookcase to our right opened, and out walked Malcolm Luxx from a secret entrance. *Sneaky bastard.*

"Mr. Luxx, how nice to see you." I extended my hand, but he didn't take it. Instead, he went over to the corner table to make himself a drink. He didn't offer me one, which meant he wasn't planning on talking to me long.

"Mr. Brooks, I thought I'd made it clear to you that I did not require your services?" Malcolm didn't look at me at all, focusing on putting round ice cubes into his glass.

"Yes, well—" I began.

"If I wanted a woman in my life, I assure you, I wouldn't need to pay for her company."

"Understood." I had to think fast. He was giving me the brush-off. "Which is why I'm here not as a businessman, but as a friend to celebrate your birthday. I've even brought you a gift."

At that, Malcolm looked up at me. "A gift?"

I grabbed Amanda's waist and moved her gently toward him. "The use of Amanda for the night, free of charge—a service I never provide with my pets. However, since it's your birthday..."

"I'm not interested."

"A week?"

Malcolm opened his mouth to object, but there was a slight hesitation there. He was considering it. I needed to make this worth his while. He merely needed a taste of what a pet could offer, then there would be no price he wouldn't pay to keep her—and position himself to be easily manipulated into future business deals.

"Two weeks," I amended, seeing him shifting his weight. "If, after two weeks, you find Amanda's services are not beneficial to you, I'll take her back—no questions asked."

Malcolm took a sip from his drink, as he looked at Amanda over the rim of his glass. *I had him.* I fucking had the bastard. It was an offer too good to pass up. Plus, it would also be a good test for me, to see if I could be apart from Amanda for two weeks. If I could, I'd charge him through the nose, accordingly. If I couldn't, then I'd renege my offer and take her back. It was perfect.

"And if I tire of her after a day?"

I fought back my smile. He wouldn't. "I'm a call away. I will remove her, and see that she is properly punished for not living up to your expectations." I felt Amanda squirm in my grasp. My fingers dug into her flesh, a warning to stay silent.

"And what does the woman think of such an arrangement?" Malcolm asked, walking over to Amanda. She kept her eyes focused on the wall behind Malcolm and didn't say a word. *Good girl.*

"Her opinion hardly matters," I said.

"It matters to me," Malcolm insisted. "Tell me—Amanda, is it? What are your *honest* thoughts about being loaned out to a total stranger for two weeks? To be made to do anything and everything that I desire?"

Amanda didn't speak, or even breathe.

"You may answer, Amanda," I said. My fingers still dug deeper into her side.

"I would be honored, Master."

Malcolm looked at me. "Master? That's a little barbaric, don't you think?"

"You can command her to call you whatever you wish. She will answer to your every whim."

Malcolm looked again at Amanda. I watched as his eyes darted quickly down to her chest, hovering there a bit too long, before moving back up to her eyes. Without prompting, my free hand balled into a fist, ready to pummel him for sneaking a peek at *my* pet...except she wasn't. I was actively looking to adopt her into Malcolm's care. *Why had I reacted so impulsively?*

"Two weeks? What's the catch?" Malcolm asked. I relaxed my hand. His interest was piqued.

"No catch. Just trying to close a tough sale," I said, smiling. "Two weeks should provide you ample time to see if she's a good fit for you and your needs. Bring her out for a test drive, so to speak."

Malcolm looked at Amanda longingly. I knew that look all too well: it was the same one I had given her earlier today. Not that I could fault the man for looking—she was a prize. Still, something about the twitch of his lips made me want to haul off and punch him for such disrespect. I had to shake myself out of the thought.

"And the weapon at her ankle?" Malcolm asked.

"Weapon?"

"I have metal detectors at the entrance. We know she's carrying something. My guards are right outside the door, waiting for my command, should you try something foolish."

I raised my hands, knowing he was doing his best to assert dominance. "It is not a weapon. It's an ankle monitor."

At that, Malcolm lifted an eyebrow.

"It's for your protection—this way she's not a flight risk. Would you like me to show you?" I offered, taking a step toward Amanda.

"No. Let her show me."

Amanda's eyes found mine, waiting for permission. "It's okay. Show him that you aren't a threat."

With slightly shaky fingers, Amanda bent and slowly pulled

down the zipper of her boot, exposing her gorgeous calf and one perfectly harmless monitor.

"If she runs, I'll know it, and she'll be stopped before you're ever implicated. Our top priority is owner satisfaction." I beamed at him.

Malcolm surprised me by scoffing. "It doesn't seem like your pets are as housebroken as you claim them to be. Ankle monitors? Who wants to fuck someone with that on their leg? I think we're done here," he said, with a bored tone.

"If you would prefer her to not wear one, it can be removed—but if she should escape, that's not on me."

"I have ample security," Malcolm said, gesturing to his bank of monitors, "or haven't you noticed?"

"That you do," I said, grinding my teeth. It was true, Malcolm had one of the finest security setups around, far more than my average client. So be it. I could track Amanda in other ways. Not worth blowing a sale over. "The monitor will be removed. Do we have a deal, then? "I watched closely as Malcolm took a step toward Amanda. He reached out a hand and traced a thumb over her bottom lip.

Hook, line, and sinker.

"That depends."

"On?" I asked.

"On if Amanda would like to stay with me for two weeks."

I fought a smile. "Amanda, do you consent to stay with Malcolm for two weeks, obeying him as your master as you have obeyed me?"

"Yes, Master."

Her words, while exactly what I'd demanded, still stung me. How quickly she'd be in the arms of another man...

"Your two-week trial begins now, then," I said, reaching out a hand to shake on it.

Malcolm didn't move his eyes off Amanda. "Remove the monitor, then remove yourself from my property."

If this sale wasn't so important, I might have gutted him right then and there for being so disrespectful to me. Biting back my fury, I pulled out the key from inside my jacket pocket, then knelt and removed Amanda's monitor. I gave her ankle one soft squeeze.

Please don't run. I don't want to have to kill you.

"You may go," Malcolm said, just as I was about to give Amanda her final instructions. My hands balled into fists. This was a power play. Malcolm was itching to assert his dominance over her. As a master myself, I understood the urge, despite my objection to tell him to fuck off. Knowing a sale might be on the line, however, I allowed his order to stick, and merely glanced once at Amanda— in both warning and longing.

If he returned her after two weeks, would I be upset or relieved?

CHAPTER TWENTY-THREE

Amanda

Stunned by how quickly Connor had given me away to a stranger without any sort of payment, I stood there, frozen. His semen was still dried on the inside of my thighs, but he'd abandoned me like I was nothing.

It dawned on me, then, how disposable I was to him. He didn't care about me. I was an idiot. Instead of being thrilled at having left my cage, I was hurt because my captor didn't want me? Jesus, that was messed up. Connor was right—he was a monster, but so was I. I'd fallen prey to yet another twisted man's fetishes. I deserved whatever fucked-up treatment Malcolm was about to dish out.

But what, exactly, was he going to do with me for two weeks? While I knew "Malcolm" to be Dayton from high school, I did not recognize the man looking back at me. Dayton had been a quiet kid, scared and on edge, always looking over his shoulder. This man towered over me, commanding the room. Even Connor, strong as he was, seemed to cower in his presence. There was no telling what he would do to me. It might pale in comparison to Connor's treatment.

Not knowing what else to do, I played it as safe as I could and got to my knees, then lowered my head, waiting for orders. Better to be obedient and assess my situation, than to be defiant and risk getting hurt.

"Stand up," Malcolm ordered, almost disgusted. "You don't need to do that for me."

I looked up and saw him extending his hand to help me up. Confused, I took it. When I was upright, he didn't release my hand. Instead, he placed a finger to his lips as he walked us to the door and closed it, sliding a deadbolt into place. I swallowed hard. He'd locked us in. Panic set in and I took an instinctual step backward.

Malcolm noticed my withdrawal and let my hand go, walking over to a bank of security cameras. "I'm not going to hurt you, Amanda," he said. "I want to make sure he's gone before I take you out of here."

I didn't know what he meant by that. Did he intend to bring me to his bedroom—surely, he wouldn't want to sleep with me while he had a house full of people? Then again, I had no idea what this man's kink was. My skin ran cold as my eyes fell to the floor. "Yes, Master."

"No! Don't call me that. I'm not your master." My eyes widened, and I shrunk back in fear. At once, Malcolm's voice lowered. "Nor are you anyone's slave."

I looked up at him, confused. "I don't understand what you want me to do."

His face crumpled into an expression I couldn't quite place. "Amanda, I don't want any..." His fingers pinched the bridge of his nose, and closed his eyes. "Do you remember me?"

So Malcolm *did* recognize me—that was a good sign. Maybe he'd be kinder? Then again, when had a man ever been kind to me?

"How could I forget Dayton Littlefield?" I admitted.

Malcolm's jaw flexed. "I haven't used that name since I was a teenager." He shook his head, as though trying to push away a bad memory, then pointed toward one of the screens showing Connor leaving the house. "What are you doing with that vile man?"

It was an odd feeling, watching Connor go—relief and sorrow all mixed into one. "I wasn't with him by choice."

"Did he kidnap you?" There was an edge to Malcolm's voice.

"Trapped me is a better word for it. He lured me into his building under the guise of a rental unit. Once I was inside...that was it. The doors were locked and there was no escape. He's got the whole floor rigged up like cells, maybe the whole building. I don't know how many girls he has there, but it's a lot."

"The bastard." Malcolm came over to me and looked me dead in the eyes. "Did he hurt you?"

"Nothing more than I'm used to." I shrugged. "I seem to have a way of pissing people off."

Malcolm's lips curled into a slight smile. "I remember. You had quite the mouth on you, if I recall."

I laughed. "Some things never change, I guess...well, except you. New name, new attitude, new body." I gestured toward his physique. "I would've never predicted that the boy I knew back then would become as successful as you have."

"Successful," he huffed. He went to the monitors and watched for a moment, this time looking at the gated entrance. I could make out taillights. "He's gone." Malcolm turned to face me. "You're safe here. I won't hurt you, I promise."

"Are you going to buy me?"

He recoiled. "*Buy* you? No, I will not finance that devil's pocketbook." Walking over to a desk, he pulled out a drawer and removed what looked like a banker's bag. "But I will set you free. I'll take you to a safehouse, hook you up with a new identity, and—"

"No!" I cried. Malcolm looked at me as though I'd grown two heads. He didn't understand the power Connor had. I had only caught a glimpse of it, and I knew enough then to attempt to cheat that man. "You have to buy me or return me—that's the only way he'll back off. In fact, maybe it's best if you return me. After he's punished me for failing to satisfy you, I think I can convince him to keep me as his own personal pet."

Malcolm looked at me, horrified. "You *want* to go back to him?"

"This isn't about what I want," I said. "There are other women trapped in that complex, and they're being sold off too. I think that if I can get Connor to trust me, I can figure out some way to save them."

"Amanda, you can't save them. If you go back, he'll sell you to someone else."

"I don't think he will, though. I don't even think he wanted to see you tonight. I think..."

"What?"

"I think Connor likes me. I think he wants to *keep* me. If I went back, maybe I could get him to tell me something I could hold over him...or figure out how to get the others out."

"Or get yourself killed," Malcolm said. "Look, I appreciate the attempt to save the other women, but you can't save them from inside a prison. Let me take you somewhere safe, and then I'll see if there's anything I can do."

"But—"

He raised a hand and I flinched, thinking he was going to hit me. Malcolm recoiled immediately, taking a step back. "I'm not going to hurt you Amanda, but this is not up for discussion. I have a house. It's private, secluded. I'll set you up there. You'll be safe."

"And what happens in two weeks? What happens when he comes back for me, and I'm not here?"

Malcolm shrugged. "He'll be returning to an empty house. He can't be angry at me if he can't find me."

"So the plan is to steal his property? That's suicide!" I shrieked. "You don't get it—he'll punish the other girls when he finds out what you did. He's that twisted. And then, he'll send his goons to look for me. If he can't find me, he'll find anyone I've ever been in contact with, and hurt them too. That includes you. He won't stop. If you don't plan to buy me, send me back. *Please*," I begged, sinking to my knees.

"Hey, hey, it's okay, Amanda," Malcolm soothed. "He's not

going to find you, or me. No one knows where this house is, not even my assistants. I'm a very private person when I want to be."

I shook my head. "It doesn't matter how private you think it is. He'll find you, and he'll kill us. *He will kill us*. Do you get that?"

Malcolm's jaw tensed as he took a step closer to me. "Amanda, I think you underestimate my security systems."

"It won't be enough. Connor has connections. If you double-cross him...if you take something that belongs to him...just send me back. I can't risk you getting involved."

Malcolm looked at me for a moment, then went over and picked up the phone on his desk. "Get the Tahoe," he said into it. I sighed in relief.

"Thank you," I said. "Taking me back to him is the right move."

After he hung up, Malcolm held out his hand. "We'll leave shortly."

"A Tahoe, huh?" I asked. "I figured you for a Cadillac sort of guy."

"The Tahoe is bulletproof. Now, let me at least get you some new clothes. I can't imagine a dress that tight is comfortable."

I arched an eyebrow. "You have women's clothing in my size in your house? Wait, let me guess, you have a mall or something in the basement?"

He frowned. "No, but I do have some workout gear you should be able to fit into."

"That does sound better than this. Hell, *any* clothes would be a welcome change after the last few days I've had."

"He didn't provide you with clothing?"

I flinched at the memories. "I'd rather not get into it. The less you know, the safer you are. I'll stay in this. Otherwise, you likely won't get your clothes back."

"Do you sincerely think I care if a pair of sweatpants and a hoodie make it back to me?" Malcolm gestured around his opulent surroundings. "What's important to me is that my guests feel comfortable."

Nodding, I let him lead me out of his study and into his bedroom.

That was my first mistake.

MALCOLM

While Amanda showered and changed into the garments I had laid out for her in the master bath, I texted Camila.

> Code Blue. I need provisions for two in the Tahoe in twenty minutes. And clear my schedule for the next month. Maybe two.

I waited for her to question my orders even though she knew better than to pry, especially with a Code Blue. That told her all she needed to know: I had to disappear in a hurry, and all traces of my whereabouts needed to be erased. In my years in the black market, I'd only had to use the Code Blue twice, and it was the one thing that had ensured my survival.

The dots bobbed up and down on the other end before her reply came.

> Consider it done. You two have fun. ;)

Camila's insinuation was clear but unwarranted. I was doing this to protect Amanda, not as some romantic getaway. Just because she and Darcy wanted me to find someone didn't mean that I did. I was a dangerous man who worked a dangerous job. Romance was not in the cards for someone like me, and I'd made my peace with it.

I deleted the text thread, as would she. Though it would still show on our phone records, that line was registered under an alias. Camila would pack up the house after we'd left and see that my affairs were handled. The party would continue without me, and then the guests would be politely asked to leave within the hour so that I could "paint"—my clientele was used to bowing to the inspiration of such a beloved artist. If only they knew they were technically buying art from unknowns.

I left my phone on top of the bureau. Camila would come wipe it and destroy it. New burner phones would be in the vehicle, along with whatever she could come up with for Amanda in such a short window. Bags were always packed for me, but I'd never once taken a guest on such an outing, let alone had one in my bedroom.

There wouldn't be enough time to get Amanda on board with my plan to move her to the safehouse—it was better to let her think she was going back to that deviant than tell her the truth. I would no sooner send a stray cat back into that Connor's hands, let alone the woman I'd fantasized about throughout my formative years. If she couldn't see past helping those other women to ensure her own safety, I would do it on her behalf. I would honor my word —I'd hide Amanda, keep her safe, *and* find a way to help the others Connor had trapped without compromising my own less-than-legal goings-on.

How, exactly, was a problem for another day.

The issue at hand was getting Amanda as far away from Connor as fast as I could, before he changed his mind and reneged on his arrangement. If I could use that two-week window to my advantage, I might be able to find a fast solution to the problem— but if he turned up on my doorstep tonight looking to change the terms of the deal, there wouldn't be much I could do besides buying Amanda outright, which was not only morally wrong, but would give Connor the upper hand. He'd hold that over my head for the rest of my life, and, by extension, maintain his control over Amanda. If he was as crazy as she said, he would never let her go... not that I could blame him. If she were mine, I'd never let her go, either.

That's when the bathroom door opened, and Amanda came out. She had on my gray sweats and a white t-shirt two sizes too big for her. Her hair was dripping onto the shirt, causing her nipples to become slightly visible through the fabric. I had to look away before I got hard. How could a woman wearing workout gear be so alluring? I focused my attention on putting my wallet into my suit jacket. "The car will be ready shortly. Do you need anything to eat or drink?"

She laughed. "I'd kill for a Big Mac."

"A Big Mac?" I asked. "Wow, I haven't had one of those since high school."

Amanda's eyes softened. "I remember. You used to love them. You had them all the time for lunch."

I cocked my head. "How do you know that?"

She shrugged sheepishly. "I used to envy you. Every day, you'd pull out a Big Mac, while I had to settle for the free school lunch of slop. I was so jealous. I thought you must have been so rich to have that every day. And look—you are." She laughed.

"I wasn't rich then. Far from it. My mom worked the night shift at McDonald's. She got a free meal, but she always gave it to me. Those burgers were *awful* cold. I envied your slop—at least it was warm."

"I had no idea," she said.

"That was the point."

"We were a lot more alike back then than we realized."

"Perhaps." I took one last look at my bedroom before plastering on a smile. "Come, the car will be waiting for us." I held out my hand, surprised when she slipped her delicate hand inside of mine. As gently as I could, I led her out of my house and down to the lower level. She would not leave my sight from this moment on, no matter how much she protested. This was for her own protection.

CHAPTER TWENTY-FOUR

Amanda

A few minutes later, Malcolm escorted me out of his sprawling house to his parked Tahoe inside a four-car garage. Three other cars, all black, filled the other bays. The windows of the Tahoe were tinted as only the rich could get away with. He opened the door to the back seat, and I raised an eyebrow.

"I don't get to ride shotgun?"

Malcolm ground his teeth. "I don't want anyone seeing us leave together. Get in, and stay low."

"The windows are tinted," I pointed out.

"Get in the car, Amanda."

We had a mini stare-down, but I finally relented. He wanted to protect his reputation, and didn't want to be seen with what people would assume was an escort. It made sense, but it was still annoying.

Once I was seated in the back, Malcolm pointed to the floor. "On the ground. I have cameras everywhere once we leave the garage. No one can suspect you're in this vehicle."

"You sure know how to treat a lady," I grumbled, getting onto the floor. At least it was clean—not like my own car would be if I had one. He must have people to tend to the details like this. I couldn't see Malcolm in here with a Dustbuster.

He closed the door behind me and slid into the front seat. The garage door opened, letting in light from outside, and the locks engaged as the car moved forward. "Once we're clear, you can move up front, but for now, stay down."

"Yes, Master," I sighed.

"Don't call me that."

"Sorry. It's kind of been drilled into me lately."

Malcolm was quiet a moment as the car navigated out of the garage. I bumped and jostled along with the bags in the trunk. "How long has he been holding you?" he asked.

I shifted my body, curving my legs better around the middle console. "Only a few days, but he doesn't give you anything to mark time with. Part of his process. He wants you disoriented. Some of the women have been in there for months, though." I shook my head. "Which is why bringing me back is the smart move. I think I can get Connor to trust me, and I think it's working too. He's already let me sleep in his bed, something he said he never lets his pets do."

"You slept in his bed?" Malcolm's voice was laced with judgment.

"We did a lot more than sleep. Spoiler alert, we had sex. A lot of it. And before you get all high and mighty with me," I said, "it's not like I had much of a choice. It was either I submit to his commands, or he'd torture one of the other women. Well, probably me, too, but the others would pay for my refusal to give him what he wanted. So yes, I had sex with him. Judge me all you want, but I wasn't about to see someone suffer for my benefit."

"He raped you, Amanda. That wasn't sex. Don't confuse the two."

I shrugged. "Or it's just my pattern. It's not the first time I've slept with his sort. It's kind of my thing." I hated how true that was.

"Don't do that, Amanda. Don't try to lessen the torment he put you through. What Connor did was wrong, plain and simple."

"Was it though? I mean, it's not like I fought him off. Plus, he's not hard on the eyes."

Malcolm was quiet as he processed my words. "Did you...enjoy it? The sex with Connor?"

There was the ten-million-dollar question. "I'm as much of a monster as he is if I say 'yes,' right?"

"I didn't say that."

"You didn't need to." I sighed as my fingers traced the edge of my t-shirt. "Look, I know this situation is messed up. Yes, the sex was good. It was great, actually, best of my life. And yes, I know how fucked up that is, so don't give me a lecture, okay?"

He didn't say anything. He probably pitied me and how stupid I was, but there was no point in lying. I *did* enjoy the sex we had, I *did* know how demented that made me. It didn't change the facts, though.

"It's not your fault, Amanda. You're experiencing Stockholm Syndrome," Malcolm said after a moment. "I know it's been debunked as an actual diagnosis, but the logic is there. It's a defense mechanism, the mind's way of navigating trauma: turn the nightmare into something positive. Turn the terror into love."

I laughed weakly. "That about sums up every relationship I've ever had. But it also might be that Connor has a great body and knows how to fuck."

I listened for Malcolm's response, but he didn't say anything for the longest time. Then, finally, he asked an impossible question.

"Do you love him?"

"No," I replied. "I mean, am I turned on by him? A thousand percent—he's that sexy and gets me off in ways no other man has. But I'm also not stupid. I know this isn't love, not in the way it's meant to be. But it might be the closest thing I'll ever get so... beggars can't be choosers." I could tell this conversation was making him uncomfortable, so I changed the subject. "What about you? You ever been in love?"

"Unrequited, so it doesn't count."

"Ouch. What happened?" I asked, hurting on his behalf. I knew how hard that sucks.

"It wasn't her fault. She didn't know I existed," he said, voice laced with regret.

"Man, do I know that feeling."

"You do?" he laughed. "I find it hard to believe anyone not returning your affections."

I sat up and leaned against the door, being sure to keep my head low. "You didn't." I tugged at the edge of my hoodie while he processed my confession.

The car slowed a moment as we approached a stop, probably at the gate.

"What do you mean?" Malcolm asked once the car started moving again.

"You ignored me in high school. I had the biggest crush on you, but you never looked my way. Not once. I was invisible to you."

"You were *never* invisible to me, Amanda." His words thrummed with both pain and anger, sending a chill up my spine. "I knew your schedule better than you did: English in Room 213 with Mrs. Garret, Bio in the Green Wing with the ever-changing substitute, Gym, Lunch, Chemistry upstairs with Mr. Macke, US History with Mrs. Joyce, and then Art with Ms. Edna," he recited.

I felt a smile dance across my lips. "We had art together. I remember you used to lean over your canvas to study your progress with such intensity it made me jealous. You never looked at me like that. And when you loaded your palette, you'd hold the paintbrush between your teeth. Man, I never wanted to be a paintbrush more in my life."

"I...I had no idea..."

I sighed. "I know. God, I had so many sexual fantasies with you in the leading role, if you must know. I imagined how good you would be with those long artist fingers. But before I had the courage to talk to you, you moved. I was crushed."

"I—you never said anything. You never even made eye contact," he argued.

"Neither did you, pal."

"I wish I had known."

Tugging on the sleeves of my shirt, I felt myself blushing. "What would you have done if I *had* spoken to you?"

"Honestly, I probably would have passed out. If I had known, I would have begged my mom not to take that management job in New Hampshire. Screw paying the rent—Amanda Jackson knew my name!" He laughed.

"It was a very sad senior year without you there," I confessed.

"It wasn't bliss starting over in a new high school either, but it's probably good you didn't know me then. I had a major growth spurt, grew like a foot and a half in the span of three months. My mom couldn't keep me in clothes that fit, and I had terrible acne. I was all limbs and breakouts—*so* many breakouts. Consider yourself spared."

"Ah, puberty. Well, it looks like you filled out nicely."

"Right back at you," he said softly.

My cheeks filled with color. *Dayton Littlefield had liked me back.* It was hard to fathom.

Once we'd been on the road a few minutes, I peeked out the window to see if the coast was clear. It seemed like we were past the mansion's gated entrance and on the highway. "Hey, can I come up front yet?"

"Oh, yeah. Sorry. We're in the clear now."

Pushing off the floor, I climbed over the center console and plopped into the leather seat beside him. Clicking the seatbelt into place, I looked out the window, trying to get my bearings, but I had no idea where we were. Since I'd been drugged on the way to Malcolm's, I had no clue where *anything* was.

"I assume you know where you're going?"

I noticed Malcolm's eyebrows pinch together. "Yes, I know where we're going. Why don't you close your eyes and rest."

"Rest? Do you live that far from Connor's? Damn," I whispered, "how long was I out for?"

"Out for?" Malcolm asked looking over at me.

I glanced out the window. "He drugged me so I wouldn't know where you lived."

"He *drugged* you?" There was an edge to his voice that made my hair stand on end.

"I told you, he's dangerous."

"You never have to see him again," Malcolm said, turning his attention back onto the road.

"Um, yeah I will. You're driving me back to him." I laughed. That's when I saw the road sign that said we were leaving the state. "Malcolm...where are you taking me?"

"You should rest. We have a long drive."

Fuck. He wasn't taking me to Connor's, he was taking me to his safehouse. That was why he didn't want me to be seen in the car—he didn't want any of Connor's thugs to see me leave with him.

"Malcolm, no. You can't hide from him. He'll find you—"

"And if he does," Malcolm said, his tone even, "I'll be ready for him." He lifted his suit jacket to reveal a gun at his side. "He's never going to lay a finger on you again, Amanda. *Ever.*"

The conviction in his voice was almost enough for me to believe him. Almost.

He didn't know Connor the way I did. Once he found out that Malcolm had double-crossed him, it would be the end. Of both of us.

MALCOLM

I probably shouldn't have tipped my hat so fast, but I hated lying to her, and there was only so much longer I could have kept up the ruse. Amanda wasn't blind. She could see where we were going.

"Malcolm, you need to turn around. Please, I don't want you to get hurt because of me," Amanda begged as I kept my eyes split between the road and the rearview mirror, checking for cars that might be following us. So far, nothing looked suspicious.

"I've noted your concern, and I've weighed the choices," I told her. "I'm not sacrificing you to that man. If you don't want to go to the safehouse with me, that's understandable. You don't know me that well. I'll get you set up somewhere a few states away, find you a new ID, a passport, and get you some cash—"

"And how does that help hide *you*? How are you going to avoid being caught by him?"

"Amanda, you seem to fail to understand that I've been avoiding people like Connor for much of my adult life. Staying off the radar is part of my job—and if he does find me, I know how to protect myself. I'm always armed."

"So is he," she huffed, "and he's unhinged, so he has an advantage. I'm telling you, the smartest play here is to return me. It's the best shot of not only bringing Connor down, but saving those girls."

"The answer is no, Amanda. I won't do it. I won't." My voice was firm as I locked eyes with her for a moment. She appeared to hold her breath, but eventually, her shoulders dropped, and she sighed.

"It's been nice knowing you," she said.

For the next twenty minutes or so, neither of us spoke as the miles ticked on behind us. With each passing road sign, however, Amanda's tension seemed to lift. I could tell she was terrified of running, but staying was not an option, nor was buying her. Sure, I worked in the black market, but the types of crimes I'd be charged with would be mostly fines and maybe some light jail time. Participating in a human trafficking ring was next-level disgusting, a bar I refused to sink to. I'd get Amanda out of Connor's clutches, and, given enough time, he'd either forget all about us or get busted—the latter, if I had any say on the matter.

Sure, he'd probably hunt us for a while. His ego would insist upon it. But if cops started sniffing around his operation, he'd be forced to refocus his energy. That was the tentative plan: distract and detain. I had two weeks to make sure Amanda was off the grid —plenty of time to get to the safehouse, get my work affairs in order, and start the anonymous leaks to lead the officials to Connor.

"Where are we going?" Amanda asked, eventually.

"It's better if you don't know, that way you can't accidentally give anything away."

Amanda looked at me and cocked her head. "You know that I'm in the passenger's seat. I can literally see where you're driving."

I nodded once. "For now. Once we reach a certain point, I'll be asking you to wear a blindfold."

Amanda raised an eyebrow. "You want me to wear a blindfold? Seriously?"

"It's better than drugging you, isn't it?" I could see her brow rising in defiance. "Look, I don't love the idea either," I continued, "but Connor's methods, while twisted, are logical. The less you know where you're being kept, the safer it is."

"Safer for you," she muttered.

"Safer for both of us. Look, I know I haven't earned this right, but you have to trust me."

Amanda shook her head softly and leaned against the glass. "Is this not your first time kidnapping a sex slave, then?" she spat.

"Amanda, you're not a sex slave."

"Aren't I?" Her voice cracked. "I'm not worth all of this. Just leave me on the side of the road somewhere. I'll be fine." Her voice sounded so dejected, so resigned to her fate.

My teeth ground together as I pressed on the gas harder. "You'll get out of this car only when I say you get out."

"Yes, Master," she muttered.

"Amanda, *please* don't call me that."

"Then don't treat me like your captive. 'You'll get out only when I say you get out.' I mean, seriously? How are you any better than Connor?"

Damn. She was right. I was no different. Not if I was forcing her choices on her.

Pulling into the breakdown lane, I slowed the car. Coming to a full stop, I put it into park and turned to look at her. She had tears welling in her eyes, but seemed to be working hard to keep them from falling.

"You're right." I admitted. "I shouldn't have said that, nor should I be making choices about what's best for you. If you want to go back to the devil you know, I'll turn the car around right now. I'll tell Connor that it was nothing you said or did, but that I'm just not into the human trafficking thing."

Amanda's expression seemed to be assessing if I was being truthful or trying to manipulate her.

"Or you can get out of the car now, and try your luck at starting over on your own terms," I continued. "I'll tell Connor that I set you free—that you fought me tooth and nail, but I released you without your consent, so that if he does find you, you have an out."

"Are you serious?"

I took a long breath. "Yes. Amanda, I won't force you to come with me if you'd rather be with him. You are your own person. You get to make your own choices, even if I disagree with them. Now, do you want me to bring you back to him?"

Her head began to nod, and my heart sank. Connor had his hooks in her, had brainwashed her into thinking that he cared. I was too late. Sighing, I put my hands back on the wheel, and was about to pop it into drive when her hand reached out and covered mine.

"Wait," Amanda said. "I want you to take me to the safehouse. I'll wear a blindfold—I'll even blow you while you drive us. Don't make me go back there, okay?"

Her words made my heart lift. "You will never have to see that man again, not if I have anything to say about it," I said, taking her hand in mine and giving it a small squeeze.

"Thank you," she whispered, finally letting those caged tears fall.

Pulling back onto the highway, Amanda kept my hand in hers as she watched the road behind us disappear into the past. She was trusting me to keep her safe, and I would—even if it was the last thing I ever did.

CHAPTER TWENTY-FIVE

Amanda

Malcolm drove down the highway in the dying sunlight, keeping my hand in his for the better part of an hour. Never once did he try to take it back, nor did I. It was strange—holding his hand felt normal. *Right*. Like it was meant to be there. Two halves coming together to fit with perfect ease. His touch was calming. Assuring. Steady. Which was nuts. Sure, we'd gone to school together a million years ago, but we weren't friends. We didn't know each other. Why would I feel this level of safety with him?

That's when it dawned on me: Malcolm didn't seem to want anything from me—sexually, that is. He hadn't hit on me, or said anything sexual once we had escaped from Connor's watchful eye. He'd been putting on a show back then, but since Connor left, he'd been kind to me...which got me curious.

"Malcolm, can I ask you something? It might come across as crass, but I swear there's a point to the question."

He shifted in his seat a second, his square jaw tensing as he checked all of his mirrors. Once Malcolm seemed satisfied that it was okay to let his attention slide to me, he nodded, still keeping his eyes glued to the road.

"What's your question?"

I watched his face carefully, ready to capture his reaction. I knew it would be a blink-and-you-miss-it moment, so I wanted to be ready. "Do you want to fuck me?"

"What?" His eyes widened to shock before he turned to look at me. He almost seemed offended by the question, which was interesting. I tried to dig a little deeper.

"I mean, obviously not right this second while you're driving, but like, in general. Do you want to screw me? If given the opportunity, that is."

"Amanda, I don't know why you're asking me that. If I said something to imply—"

"Just answer it. I won't be mad either way, promise. It's important."

"What could possibly be gained from knowing that?"

Amanda shrugged. "I'll explain it after I get your answer. Do you want to fuck me?"

"Amanda," he scolded.

Annoyed that he was dodging the question, I lifted my hoodie and showed him my bare breasts. "What about now? Do you want to nail me?" I shook the girls for good measure.

"Jesus, Amanda, pull your shirt down!"

"Why? The windows are tinted, right? No one can see me."

"I can," he huffed.

"So breasts aren't your thing. Are you an ass man?" I reached for my waistband, but then paused. "Oh, shit, are you gay?" I glanced casually down at his lap, and saw that his pants had tented slightly. "Oh, never mind. Tits it is."

"Amanda, please, I'm trying to drive."

"Then answer the question. If I spread my legs to you right now, would you sleep with me?"

Malcolm's face was getting red. He was clearly aroused, despite trying not to be, but he wouldn't look at me or my breasts. He kept his eyes on the road. "No, Amanda, I don't want to *fuck* you."

At that, I pulled down my shirt, feeling oddly dejected. "Wow. That might be a first for me."

He didn't say anything for a moment, as his woody slowly

softened. "Well, I'm not everyone," he admitted. "Women are respected in my world. Cherished. Lavished. They are not objects for my amusement, okay? I don't *fuck* them."

"So what—you're one of those guys who 'makes love?'"

He looked me dead in the eyes, causing me to shiver slightly. "Yes, I am."

"Okay...would you ever make love to me?"

His sigh almost sounded like regret. "Only if you loved me. But therein lies the rub—I am not a loveable man. Okay? Can we drop the subject now?"

"Okay," I whispered, too stunned to say more than that. It wasn't just what he said, it was the way he said it. Like it pained him.

Malcolm was dead silent, adjusting his mirror unnecessarily. His eyes kept checking behind him, making me wonder if we were being followed, even though there were no cars behind us. "We're about to drive through a long stretch of nothingness for a bit." He gestured to the straight road ahead. "You should close your eyes, try to get some sleep."

"Is that code for you not wanting me to see where we're going?"

At that, he frowned. "No, I've decided I am not going to make you wear a blindfold. You should know where we're going—otherwise, I'm no better than Connor. I've got a cabin in the woods. Completely secluded. Off the grid. We'll be safe there."

"A cabin in the woods. Cool," I said. "Is it in Washington? Oregon?"

He flinched. "New Hampshire."

"New Hampshire?" I shrieked. "You're driving me across the country?"

"Like I said, you might want to get some rest. We're going to be driving a while."

My mouth was still open in shock. A trip like this would take days. It was one thing for Malcolm to stash me away somewhere a few hours away from his house, but driving across the country was ridiculous.

"Would you prefer someplace warmer?" he asked suddenly. "I have a place in Miami, and one in St. Louis, but they aren't as secure. I'd need time to amp protections up, if you'd—"

"Why?"

He glanced over at me. "Why what?"

"Why are you volunteering to do this for me? You're disrupting your whole life for a perfect stranger."

"You're not a stranger. We went to high school together." He smiled.

"You know what I mean," I said, crossing my arms over my chest. "This is a major thing you're doing. I guess I don't get why you're going through this much effort to help me."

"Honestly," Malcolm sighed, "I don't know why, either." His eyes looked tired—no, not just his eyes, his whole body seemed worn out. "I can't send you back to him. I just can't. If that means a few days in a car with you, and a break from everything, then so be it. A small price to pay."

"Small price?" I laughed. "I wouldn't even be able to afford the gas for such a trip, let alone that much time away from work."

"Yes, well, I'm a wealthy man, and I'm used to traveling for what I do."

"But I have nothing to pay you back with."

He smiled once, and then looked at me. "Your company is enough. My work is normally quite solitary. So this," he gestured between us, "it's nice to have someone to talk to. That's all the payment I require." He activated the cruise control on his console, and as the engine settled in for the long stretch of road, I had a horribly naughty idea.

"Well, there's one thing I can think of to repay you," I teased.

"Honestly, you don't need to repay—Amanda! What are you doing?"

"I'm giving you head on the highway," I said, undoing his belt.

MALCOLM

Her hands were amazingly fast. Before I could even open my mouth to stop her, Amanda had me out of my pants and in her hands. I hated how quickly I'd grown hard for her. This wasn't what I wanted her to think of me.

"My God, you're fucking huge. Like, seriously massive," she said, with a level of awe that had me blushing. Still...this wasn't appropriate.

"Amanda, no. *Stop*."

She looked up at me, her hands already moving up the base of my shaft, and smiled. "Your lips say no, but your cock says yes."

It took every shred of willpower to repeat myself. "I said 'no,' Amanda."

She blinked at me. "Wait...you're serious? You don't want me to suck you off?"

"I do not." Gritting my teeth, I gently removed her hand from me. Amanda retreated from me as though she'd been struck.

Glancing into the rearview mirror, I pulled over to the side of the road, shifted into park, then made fast work of getting my dick back in my pants. Amanda curled her knees inside her sweatshirt, seeming embarrassed.

"Look, Amanda," I started, "it's not that I don't find you attractive—"

"It's fine. You don't need to explain." Her eyes darted out the window. She was uncomfortable. I'd upset her.

"Amanda, please believe me when I say that, while I would very much appreciate the offer if we were in a consensual relationship, I can't condone this action. I won't have you feeling obligated to give me sexual favors as some sort of payment for helping you out of a living nightmare. I refuse to use you. I was raised to treat women with respect, not as sexual objects at my disposal."

She shifted slightly in her seat. "So what...you respect me too much to let me give you a blow job?" she asked, with an air of condescension.

"Yes. I don't want or need payment. I need to make sure you're safe. That's it. Okay?"

I watched Amanda carefully as she absorbed my words. It was clear to me that, somehow, she'd come to determine that her value as a woman was defined by what she could give to a man. I'd have to be very careful with her in the coming days. She had to know that she was worth so much more than her physical attributes. She deserved more than the life Connor had wanted to subject her to.

After a few moments, Amanda gave me a nod. "Okay," she whispered. "Got to admit, that's the first time a guy has told me 'no.'"

Inadvertently, I shifted myself in my pants as my cock slowly eased its way back down. "Yeah, well, that's the first time I've turned a woman down. So a new experience for us both."

She smiled, but then said, "Thank you."

"Don't mention it." I put the car back into drive, and started back onto the highway. Once we were in traffic, Amanda let out a deep breath and allowed her legs to come out from the sweatshirt. I could feel her eyes on me, studying me.

"So since a blow job is off the table, and I'm too wired to sleep, why don't we talk? Tell me about you," she said. "What happened after you left Maine? I mean, I know your mom got that manager job, but how did that turn into *this*?" She gestured to the space around me.

I shrugged. This wasn't the sort of story I would tell just anyone, but we did have hours of driving ahead of us, and something about Amanda made me trust her.

"It started innocently enough," I began. "Took some advanced art classes my senior year of high school, mostly so that I didn't have to take a language—I have no mind for that sort of thing. And, I don't know, I guess I had a knack for it. Abstracts, mostly. Very few could understand what I was trying to communicate, but my art teacher could see it. She encouraged me to apply to art school. I got some financial aid, one of the few benefits of being so poor, and my career sort of took off. Fast forward a few years, and all of a sudden, everyone wanted a painting from Malcolm Luxx."

"About that," she said. "When did you change your name? I liked Dayton."

Another shrug. "That was my roommate's idea. There was already a Daniel Littlefield in my year, and our artwork was always getting mixed up because we had similar initial signatures. My roommate, Brendon, said I should have a classier sounding name. He said rich white people would buy paintings from an exotic name like "Malcolm" or "Luxx" before they'd buy it from a hick called Dayton Littlefield. So Malcolm Luxx was born. It was freeing, actually. I found that I could paint better as Malcolm. It separated me, somehow. The work came easier. By the time I'd graduated art school, I had commissions for one hundred and seven paintings. It was nuts—as were the prices they were willing to pay."

I glanced in the review mirror again. So far, it was just us on the road. I wondered how long we'd have before Connor caught wind of the double-cross. While I wouldn't hesitate to kill him if he tried to take Amanda, I also understood how much of a loose cannon he was. I had to be ready for anything.

Glancing over at Amanda, I saw she had curled her feet up on the seat so that she was hugging her knees, seeming fully engaged in my story. She hadn't picked up on my unease about how much time we had. That was good. She didn't need to be burdened with that.

"So you got rich before leaving school? That's impressive."

"Well, not rich, but I had a pretty steady future. But I was also young and stupid," I continued, "and reckless with my newfound wealth, as any guy in his twenties would be."

"Let me guess—booze, drugs, and women?" The way she said it almost sounded like she was jealous.

"Not exactly. It was more like pizza, video games, and computers. Remember, I was not very attractive then, and socially awkward. I never grew out of that one. Never properly learned how to 'people.'"

"What happened then—spend all the money?"

"The opposite, actually. I couldn't seem to spend it fast enough. The demand for my work kept growing, and I couldn't keep up with it. My ideas were getting as stale as the pizza crusts that littered my studio." I shook my head at the memory. "Then, one day, I was giving a talk at a local art school—you know, trying to give back and all—and the teacher showed me some of her students' projects. And Amanda, there was this one kid who was amazing, a gift well beyond something I could ever achieve. Similar to my stuff in tone, but leaps and bounds better. I found myself wanting to buy it from her, to study her strokes, but it wasn't for sale. She was giving it to her mother for her birthday." Pinching the bridge of my nose, I sighed. "So I broke into the school that night and stole it. I know, I know, I'm a horrible person." I raised my hands in surrender for a moment, before putting them back on the wheel. "But I wasn't going to keep it—I was going to give it back. I wanted to spend some time with it. Emulate it. My muse was thirsty for inspiration, and that one painting felt like it would be the life support it needed."

"And was it?"

"It would have been, if my art broker hadn't sold it. She'd assumed it was mine, and fetched a great price for it. The demand for more like it followed thereafter. Before I knew it, I found myself breaking into artists' homes across the globe."

"I can't imagine you breaking into a school and stealing a some poor kids' canvases."

"They weren't poor for long. They were handsomely rewarded for their work, all of them—either in large wads of cash where the paintings had been, or other career windfalls that would mysteriously come their way. I have morals...just not the muse of my youth," I said softly. "But my days of stealing art are coming to a close. I have more wealth than I know what to do with, and I

don't know...I guess I just don't have the stomach for it anymore."
He rubbed his knees. "Or the flexibility I once had."

"So it's time for a midlife crisis, huh? Where you re-kidnap a
woman and hide her away from the worst of the world?"

"Kidnap? Amanda, I'm not—"

"It was a joke." She grinned.

"Do you think I'm a horrible person for what I do?"

She shook her head. "Nah. We all do what we have to in order
to survive. God knows I've done worse."

"Oh? Like what?"

Snorting, she asked, "How much time ya got?"

I glanced at the clock on the console. "Forty-eight hours and
thirty-eight minutes."

She laughed, but seemed to comply. It was her turn to catch me
up to speed. Where had my lovely little Amanda gone in her life,
and how the hell had the Universe brought us back together again?

CHAPTER TWENTY-SIX

Amanda

Malcolm wanted to know my story, how I'd ended up in this shit show of a life. It wasn't idealistic—a sob story that would likely shift how he saw me—but maybe that would be for the best. If I was going to be stuck hiding out with him, it was probably better if he knew the real me.

"I'm not sure where to begin." I sighed. The sun was setting, and I could feel my body growing weary from the insanity of the last few days. I owed him a story, though. He'd been honest with me, and he might as well know the deal of the woman he was saving. He might decide, after hearing it, that I wasn't worth the effort.

"Tell me about what happened after I left," he volunteered as a starting point. "When did you leave Maine?"

"The day I turned eighteen." I lowered my head. "I didn't graduate. I left mid-year, on my birthday—got out of the foster system and started hitchhiking, you know? I wanted to get as far away from my life up to that point as possible. Problem was, I didn't have any skills or a degree to get a job...so to survive, I learned to barter with what I did have." My eyes darted to the window.

"Your body?"

I hated that he could see my humiliation, as my eyes closed in silent confirmation.

"I'm not judging you, Amanda. I stole kids' artwork. I'm no saint myself."

"Have you ever done something sexually with someone that you didn't want to, just so you'd be warm for a few hours, or so that you wouldn't be physically hurt?" I asked.

His eyes fell. "No, I can't say that I have."

"We are not the same." I hated how cold the words came out, but he'd asked.

"I didn't know how bad things were for you," Malcolm said after a moment. "I didn't even know you were a foster kid."

"Not many did. It's not exactly something you want to advertise. It helped that I wasn't popular at school, so I disappeared into the background pretty easily." She shrugged. "Any interest in me came from guys who seemed more interested in my boobs than my life, anyway, so I did whatever I could to keep the attention there. Away from looking at me too intensely."

"You didn't want people to know the real you?"

I shrugged, pulling my arms inside the hoodie for warmth. Or for safety. "There wasn't much to see: dead mom, drunk dad who became abusive by six, foster care in middle school, then the nomad years after I left the system that I'd rather not talk about—ever, if that's okay with you?"

"You needn't tell me anything you aren't comfortable with, Amanda."

I nodded and started picking around my nails under the shirt, something I did when I was nervous. "Eventually, I made it to Seattle. It felt about as far away from Maine as I could get. Got a job waiting tables at a crappy bar where guys groped me more than they tipped me. Lived in a bunch of shit apartments for about, oh, I don't know, eleven or twelve years? I lost track. Those years all sort of blend together. A string of on-again, off-again relationships with awful men. Then, a few years ago a new bar opened a few blocks from where I was staying. Got in there as a bartender, hoping for better tips. That's where I met Sam."

I let out a deep sigh. My whole body seemed to twist itself into knots thinking about him.

"Amanda, if you don't want to talk about—"

"No, it's fine. You should know. I have a knack for finding horrible men."

Malcolm looked over at me. I could see him raise an eyebrow in the dying sunlight. "Well, that's really not surprising, given the male role models in your life."

I snorted. "I wouldn't call my dad a role model, but I get your point. And yeah, maybe that's why I was drawn to Sam. Part of him was very much like my dad. Cocky. Confident. Cruel. My trifecta," I said, thinking of Connor. He was all three of those.

Damn, I did have a type.

"Did Sam work with you at the bar?" Malcolm asked.

I shook my head. "No, but he was there every night. That should have been a red flag. Of course, he lied and said he was there every day because he wanted to see me. He wanted the beer. I was a bonus."

I looked out the window as the streetlights zoomed by us. With each mile we drove, the tightness in my shoulders lessened. I pulled my arms back out of my sleeves and ran them over my face.

"So what happened then?"

"The usual stuff. He'd flirt with me, and I'd ignore him. It was the only way to survive a shift—ignore all the men. But I think Sam liked that I didn't pay him any attention. He took it as a challenge, and got a little more aggressive with his advances."

Malcolm's jaw tensed, and his hands gripped the wheel a little tighter. I could tell this was making him uncomfortable but there wasn't any way to sugarcoat things.

"Aggressive in what way?" he asked.

Shrugging, I started picking at my nails again. "Just verbal stuff at first, being cruder than normal. He started saying the quiet parts out loud, about what he'd like to do to me. Sexually. Right out in public where the whole bar could hear him." I shook my head. "My manager didn't do shit about it, because Sam paid his tab, and god forbid a customer ever be in the wrong." I looked out the window at the trees turning black in the darkening sky. "Then, one night, I was dropping off a beer to him, and he grabbed my wrist hard and pulled me close to his face. His tongue was in my ear before I even knew what was happening. Fucker left a bruise on my wrist, but still, nothing from management."

"He sexually assaulted you, Amanda," Malcolm fumed.

"Yeah, what else is new?"

"I don't understand—if he assaulted you, why did you end up dating him?"

I blew out a deep breath and rubbed my face a few times. "Because that's the way guys have always treated me. The next day, he apologized. Profusely. He said he'd been drunk, and he was humiliated by what he'd done. Promised it would never happen again." I laughed. "He even brought me roses and chocolates, and I don't know...no guy had ever done that before. Bought me gifts, apologized for their behavior. He begged for a chance to make it up to me. He wanted to take me to dinner...and I guess I wanted to believe that good men existed. And for a few months, he *was* kind to me—well, better to me than other men had been. He never raised his voice, he showered me with gifts, and I moved in with him. Things were finally looking up for me."

"And then?"

I let out a deep sigh. "And then, Sam started getting drunk at home instead of the bar. He could keep drinking after the last call at home. He could be loud, and sloppy, and not have to keep up his mask of pretending not to be tipsy in public. To be fair, he was only abusive when he was drunk." I shook my head. "But he was drunk a lot."

"How long were you with him?"

"Too long. I have the fractures, sprains, and broken blood vessels to prove it. The last straw, though, was when he got so shit-faced drunk that he nearly choked me to death. I was shouting so loud that I woke the neighbors. Cops came, dragged him off me, and hauled him away. While they had him in custody, I packed up and started running again. I went a few hours away—I had a friend who lived in Portland, and I was able to crash on her couch for a bit. Sam ended up getting convicted for six months, so I figured it was safe to try and lay down some roots again. But that's when I fell into Connor's trap: I went looking for an apartment. You know the rest."

"I'm so sorry you had to endure all of that, Amanda."

I shrugged. "It could be worse. I could still be with Sam. Or in that cage."

Malcolm looked over at me. "You never have to go back there. Do you hear me? I'll make sure you're safe."

I blinked at him. His words sounded so sincere...and so deadly.

"You don't owe me anything, Malcolm. Just because we knew each other when we were young, that doesn't mean you need to shift everything around in your life to make sure some lunatic doesn't get his hands on me. I'm not your responsibility. Seriously. Drop me at a rest stop. I'll be okay. I'll disappear. I'll get by. I always do."

"You'll stay with me, Amanda."

I opened my mouth to protest, but then his eyes softened.

"Please," Malcolm said, "let me get you to the safehouse. We can talk about what happens next once we're secure. Deal?"

"Why is this so important to you? Why do you care so much about what happens to me?"

Malcolm's eyes narrowed on the road. "Well, you told me your story. I might as well tell you mine."

———

MALCOLM

This wasn't a story I had told anyone. It wasn't anyone's business but mine. However, given Amanda's situation, I thought it might help her understand my motives—might convince her to stay, and not feel like she was some sort of burden on me.

"What I told you about my mom getting a management job out of state? That was true, but what was also true was that she was escaping a physically-abusive relationship. I didn't know it at first. I thought she was overtired at work and getting hurt. I didn't know it was her fucking boyfriend, Tom. I was a dumb kid who clearly wasn't putting two and two together. I knew they fought a lot, so I didn't stick around when the yelling started. I'd go out to the backyard, venture into the woods, and sort of ignore reality—learned to whittle, skip rocks, harvest mushrooms, that sort of thing. A real Maine woodsy type. All the while, my mom was being beaten, and I had no idea. Tom placed his hits strategically: never on her face. Always on her arms or torso, where a shirt would cover up the evidence. If mom moved a little slowly one day, she'd blame her arthritis or her bad back, and I believed her. I *wanted* to believe her. So I did nothing, even though I knew in my gut that something was wrong."

Amanda reached out and rested a hand on my thigh. Not in a sexual way, but as a way to show me she was listening. That she wasn't judging me. She likely understood in ways others wouldn't.

"When she told me we were moving out of state and that Tom wasn't coming with us, I didn't give her any grief. I didn't complain about leaving friends at school, because, let's be honest, I didn't have any. The only thing I felt bad about was ditching you."

"Me?" Amanda asked.

"You," I repeated. "You were the one light in my miserable high school life, but my mom needed to leave. So I had to leave you too."

"I didn't know..."

"That was the plan," I said. "I knew you could never feel the same about me, so you became this thing I could look at and never touch. And then, years later, you show up at my house as one of Connor's *pets,* and I—" Grinding my teeth together, I fought to keep my train of thought. "I couldn't let you stay with him. It was like watching Tom and my mother all over again. I could tell, just by looking at you, how scared you were. You had on the same fake smile my mother wore to try and fool everyone. I'm no longer blind to that expression now, Amanda. I see it, and I see the type of man Connor is. I knew he was dangerous, but also possessive, just like Tom, which is why we have to run. We *have* to hide. He can never be allowed to touch you again. Do you understand?"

There was a touch of hysteria to my voice that I couldn't quite mask.

"Malcolm...what aren't you telling me?"

So much for leaving that detail out of the story.

"He killed her, Amanda," I said. "My mother's psycho boyfriend, Tom, hunted her down years later and he killed her. He was biding his time until I wasn't there to protect her. I wasn't able to defend her, but so help me God, I *will* protect you. I'm not going to fail again, alright? That's why I'm moving you. That's why I need you in that safehouse. Connor is as unhinged as Tom was—worse—and I'm not letting history repeat itself. I'm not." My voice shook and I had to look away before she saw the panic behind my eyes.

"Okay," she whispered. "I'll listen to you. I'll follow your instructions."

I wanted to say "thank you," but I couldn't. There was too much emotion tightening my throat. The cycle of abuse surrounding the women I loved ended now. I would break it. I'd snap Connor's neck with my bare hands if I had to.

I would keep Amanda safe, or die trying.

CHAPTER TWENTY-SEVEN

Connor

It had only been a handful of hours since I'd dropped Amanda off with Malcolm, but I was on edge. Which was stupid. The outing couldn't have gone more perfectly. Malcolm had taken the bait, and would easily see the benefits of having a pet. I'd become richer, and would satisfy that itch of knowing I got the last laugh over that asshole. So why wasn't I happy with the outcome?

Because it had meant giving him Amanda.

"So what?" I hissed at the wall. She was nothing to me—a transaction. None of these women meant anything to me. Amanda was just great sex, that was all. That was all she could ever be to me.

Shaking my head, I tried to focus on the other tasks I'd been avoiding, like checking in on the pets. I'd done a visual scan when I'd gotten back to the building, but I preferred to do a personal check before going to sleep. I needed to make sure they were locked in before I could rest.

At Gwen's cell, I entered her room, ready to confirm she was there and then leave. She surprised me by being naked—on her knees, ass in the air.

"What are you doing?" I asked, annoyed.

"I am yours to use, Master."

I looked at her thin body, her eyes on the ground, where I'd trained them to be. It would be so easy to take her, to fuck her hard and get this tension off my shoulders...but instead of being turned on by her suggestion, I was disgusted.

"Put your clothes on, and never present yourself to me like that again."

"I'm sorry, Master," she said, scrambling to pick up her thin garment.

"For that, you'll get no food tomorrow."

Normally, I would've taken her dress away too, but I didn't want to see her naked. I didn't want to see any of them naked.

Well, all except one.

Locking Gwen back in, I completed my checks, then went back to my place and sat at my computer, pulling up my file on Amanda—including the photos that I'd taken of her on the table that first day. I stopped when I saw the I'd taken of her sitting on the table in only her panties and white a button-up blouse, her black bra showing underneath. Something about a black bra and a white blouse did it for me, my dick aching at the memory of those perfect tits, how my cock had felt tucked inside her, how her mouth had felt as she sucked me off...

My hand danced down to the edge of my pants, and soon I was jerking off to the photos I'd taken to titillate a prospective client.

When I came, I shouted Amanda's name involuntarily, shaking against the feeling of release. What the hell was this woman doing to me? She wasn't even here, and I was still thinking about her.

Kicking out of my chair, I took a shower to try and rid her from my mind. Being in the shower, however, only brought back memories of her eating her out, how delicious she had been. My mind wandered, thinking of Malcolm potentially doing the same to Amanda even now. It made my blood boil.

"Surely, he wouldn't sleep with her on the first night... would he?"

Curious, I logged onto my security system. Malcolm may have had me remove her ankle monitor, but the tracker sewn into

Amanda's dress would confirm her whereabouts. Tomorrow, I'd drop off her "things" with trackers in each outfit. I did this with all my pets, monitoring them for a few weeks after a sale to make sure they were behaving, and that the customer was satisfied.

After a few taps, the tracker pinpointed the dress to be in the northwest corner of the mansion. Pulling up the info I had on the layout of Malcolm's house, given to me by the real estate photos from the place had been on the market a few years ago, the location of the dress put Amanda in the master bedroom.

"Fuck."

Ten minutes later, I was out the door and on the way to Malcolm's with the prepped bag for Amanda in the seat beside me. As I drove, I practiced what I'd say to the help to let them grant me a conversation with Malcolm now that he was "indisposed." My foot pressed harder on the gas as I climbed the long winding hill to get to his house. The gate wasn't manned, as workers from the catering service were coming in and out at will—a security lapse if I'd ever seen one.

I parked the car in the middle of the drive and practically ran to the front door, reminding myself to walk as I got within range of the cameras. Malcolm's security team would be watching now that I was at the house. One of the catering vans was parked near the back of the house. He must have sent people home early so he could fuck her. My jaw tensed as I rang the doorbell.

For several minutes, I waited at the door for someone to answer. I even resorted to knocking. Still, nothing. I tried the handle, but it was locked. Annoyed, I went to the area where the truck was and saw the back door open as a worker came out with an armful of food trays. I slipped in behind him.

Inside, several workers were packing up the leftover food, including everything from the refrigerator—*everything*, not just what they'd served: butter, condiments, jugs of milk. *Odd.* Narrowing my eyes, I made my way into the living room and spotted the redhead from earlier. She had a clipboard in her hands, and was busy checking things off—a dominant if I ever saw one.

The snap of a bed sheet to my left caught my attention. Turning toward the sound, I saw two more workers covering the dining room table in the next room. They were closing down the house.

Why?

"Mr. Brooks, what brings you here?" The redhead was making her way over to me.

"Camila, is it? I'm here to drop this off for Amanda." I held up the duffel bag. "It's her personal belongings. I forgot to leave it with Mr. Luxx earlier. I know she'll be thrilled to get it, if you could run and snag her for me." I watched her expression carefully. She gave nothing away as glanced down at the bag, then back up at me.

"I can see that she gets it," Camila said, tucking the clipboard under her arm and holding out her hand.

"I'd rather give it to her myself."

Camila gave me a tight smile Her shoulders tensed. "I'm afraid that won't be possible. Mr. Luxx and Ms. Jackson currently indisposed."

"Indisposed?" Anger bubbled in my voice, and I tried to contain it.

"Yes, I believe he was taking her out for a drive."

"A drive, you say?" I asked as calmly as I could. I watched her face as she struggled to keep her composure. They weren't out for a drive. They were in his room not twenty feet from me, but someone was definitely getting a ride. My hands clenched into fists. "Is that so?" My eyes darted pointedly in direction of the master bedroom.

"Yes," Camila said, trying to give me the brush-off. "They did not indicate when they would return."

"So...they're currently not in the house? That's your story?"

She lifted a perfectly shaped eyebrow. "My *story?*"

My nostrils flared as I took a step forward. To her credit, she didn't budge from her spot, but I did hear her suck in a breath. She was scared of me. As she should be.

"You sure they're not in the bedroom?" I asked.

"Quite sure, Mr. Brooks. But even if they were, I'm not sure that would be any of your business."

"Not my business?" I whispered through my teeth. "Until Mr. Luxx pays me what I'm owed, Amanda is still my property."

"Property, you loaned out for two weeks, if I'm not mistaken."

I lifted a hand, ready to backhand her for speaking to me like that, but I gritted my teeth instead, remembering my place. Camila made a single hand gesture and two large men, who must have been lurking in a corner unseen, came out and flanked either side of me.

I shoved the bag at her, causing her to drop her clipboard. She scooped it up as fast as she could, but not before I got a glimpse of what was on there—three words at the top of a list: "Code Blue Evacuation."

Evacuation?

"Will that be all Mr. Brooks?" Camila asked.

"Yes," I said carefully, "that's all. See that she gets her belongings, and have Mr. Luxx call me the *second* he returns. I need his verbal confirmation that Amanda's items have been returned to her."

"Mr. Luxx doesn't do anything he doesn't wish to, sir, but I will relay your request."

Locking eyes with her one last time, I left Malcolm's house and peeled out of his driveway. From the look on Camila's face, I knew the truth: Malcolm wasn't *planning* on running. He already had. He'd taken Amanda, and not just for a drive—he'd fucking kidnapped my kidnap, had committed the cardinal sin amongst thieves. He'd stolen *my* property.

It would be the last thing he ever did. Malcolm Luxx didn't know who he was dealing with. It wouldn't matter where he took Amanda. I'd find her, and him. He had no idea what resources I had at my disposal. He would fucking pay.

Digging out my cell, I called Kenny. "Drop everything. I've got a pet adoption that's gone south. Meet me at our usual spot. Gather your best hunters for this one, yeah?"

"You got it, boss."

Soon, Amanda, I thought. Soon, I'd take back what was mine, and make sure Malcolm Luxx never saw the light of another day.

***

Thank you for reading! Please add your review because nothing helps an author more and encourages readers to take a chance on a book than a review.

And do you want to know what happens next? Find out in THE SAFEHOUSE available now. Turn the page for a sneak peek!

You can also sign up for the City Owl Press newsletter to receive notice of all book releases!

SNEAK PEEK OF THE SAFEHOUSE

For several hours, Malcolm and I didn't speak. We sat in the car as the world passed us by. Each mile marker brought me further away from the cage, but closer to uncertainty. Where were we going? And how long could we outrun a madman?

Then again, maybe I was putting too much weight on Connor's reaction to Malcolm taking me off his hands. Sure, he'd be pissed he'd been out swindled, but maybe Malcolm was right? Maybe Connor would spend some time searching for us but then give up when it became a burden to his operation. After all, I was one cog in a very big machine. Connor was smart. He wouldn't jeopardize his whole operation for me. He'd be pissed, but when we weren't easily discovered, he'd move on and I would finally be safe.

Everything was in limbo. We didn't know how long we had before Connor discovered Malcolm had taken me. Connor gave him a two-week 'trial run' with me as his pet, so in theory, we had until then to get to our safe location and hunker down until the dust settled. I was trusting that once we got to Malcolm's safehouse we'd be able to figure out if we were being hunted, and more importantly, how to help the women I'd left behind to save myself.

Glancing over at my unwitting knight in shining armor, I saw his eyes drooping. His shoulders were slumped low from hours of driving, yet his hands held the wheel with a death grip.

From the glow of the console, I could make out his strong features. His perfectly squared jaw, a dark beard trimmed close to his skin, and an expensive suit, now wrinkled. His top shirt buttons were undone, and he'd removed his tie a while ago. It was draped against the back seat, the edge of it dangling where I once hid from the threat of being discovered.

Just then, Malcolm let out a huge yawn.

"Do you want me to drive?" I asked.

"No. We'll stop at the next exit. Grab a hotel. There should be one just past the toll plaza."

"Kinky," I said, then instantly regretted it. "Sorry. Force of habit."

"It's okay. Although, I *am* going to insist we share a room. Not for that," he added quickly. "I don't want you out of my sight until we're at our final destination. If Connor is as cunning as you say he is, I don't want to take any chances."

"So, what, you'll sleep on the floor?" I raised an eyebrow.

He glanced over at me. "I'll get a room with two beds."

"Which the hotel will conveniently be out of," I said. I leaned my head on the glass.

"What?"

I shrugged. "That's how it always happens in books and movies. An attractive couple, who aren't technically a couple, try to check into a hotel with separate rooms or separate beds. But, to the shock of no one, there are no doubles available, and they just *have* to share a bed."

"I'm quite sure the motel will have the accommodations we require."

"Let's bet on it. Loser has to sleep on the floor."

He frowned. "Amanda, I'm not going to let you sleep on the floor."

"You won't need to, because I'm going to win." I stuck out my hand. He sighed, but he took my hand and gave it a small shake. He didn't let my hand go immediately, and it sent a small shiver through me.

"We'll get off at the next exit. Keep your eyes open."

I looked down at his hand as it slowly pulled away from mine. "They're open."

After the toll, he pulled off at the next exit and, sure enough, there was a hotel. Well, motel. And a crap one at that. The sign was missing two of its letters, and there was an outdoor pool that looked like it hadn't been used in years. There was a sheen of grime that peppered the outside walls. It was a place to sleep for the truly desperate or irrationally horny. Of which I was both.

"Not quite the level of luxury you're used to?" I guessed when he pulled into a spot. Malcolm frowned before he got out of the car. I followed close behind him as he made his way to the trunk to get the bags.

"On the contrary," he said. "This feels like home. Don't forget I grew up dirt poor. But more importantly, it's not where Connor would expect *me* to be, so it's perfect." He closed the trunk and locked the car. "Let's go."

Malcolm was probably right. Connor wouldn't know we'd left the house, let alone the state yet. There was no reason to feel so on edge, and yet, I couldn't help but look over my shoulder as we walked through the parking lot. There was a yellow school bus that took up nearly half of the lot. Great. Rowdy kids and a crap room. Awesome.

Malcolm was about two steps ahead of me. I watched as his eyes darted left to right as though he was scanning for danger. I was right there with him. On edge. With each car I passed, I wondered if Connor might jump out, pull me inside, and speed away before Malcolm could do anything about it. I shook my head, trying to ward off the panic.

Inside, the motel's lobby was little more than the size of a living room. On one wall, there was a small counter that held large plastic containers of assorted generic-looking cereal and a toaster. At least breakfast would be included. Not that Malcolm couldn't afford breakfast elsewhere.

There were two small tables for guests to eat at near a fake fireplace, and a couple of wooden chairs at the window. A small coffee table held heaps of curled-edge magazines. There was no one at the front desk.

"Hello?" Malcolm asked the empty room.

I noticed there was a ding bell at the counter, so I gave it a hard hit.

A moment later, a door opened near the continental breakfast nook. "Oh, hello. I didn't hear ya come in."

An older man with silver hair and a Mr. Roger's style cardigan shuffled behind the counter. His eyes blinked several times as though we'd woken him.

"It's no problem," I offered. "We're sorry to be here so late."

The man waved my apology away before he grabbed a pencil. "Checking in or do you need to book a room?"

"We need one room. Double beds. Paying with cash if that's okay?"

The man nodded and opened up a large paper ledger. There didn't seem to be any sort of computer around. "We only take cash, so you're in luck. We're a bit old school here. Thought it might lose business at first, but there is an ATM around the corner and for the most part, there seems to be a fair amount of people who don't like their whereabouts tracked on those fandangled credit card machines. I don't need Big Brother knowing my business, am I right?" He laughed. His voice was gruff like he smoked a pack a day.

"Privacy is rare these days," Malcolm agreed.

"Indeed, it is. Now, let's see what we have. Just got in a bus full of basketball kids, so they've cleaned me out pretty good. But I think I might have..." He flipped a few pages. Then flipped back one. "Well, looks like the best I can offer you is a single with a king bed. Seventy-five dollars a night. Free breakfast and coffee from five to ten a.m. That work for ya?"

I looked up at Malcolm and smiled, whispering, "'I told you 'So'" to him.

Malcolm frowned. "Are the floors carpeted?"

"They are."

"We'll take it." He slid a hundred-dollar bill at the man. "You can keep the change."

The man's eyes lit up. "Well, thank you, sir. And a name?"

"Jack—"

"Gavin. Mr. and Mrs. Gavin. We just got married. She's still not used to my name," Malcolm said. He pulled me to him and kissed the top of my head. I realized my blunder immediately.

"Damn," I said. "I need to remember that, huh?" I slid my arm around him too and stood on my tiptoes to plant a kiss on him. He froze at first but then relented and allowed the moment to happen. *Fuck.* He was a great kisser.

I only pulled away when the man at the desk cleared his throat. Malcolm held onto my bottom lip with his teeth for a second before he finally let me go.

"Sorry. Newlyweds." I blushed.

"You two enjoy your stay now," he said. I noticed he glanced down at my left hand. There was no wedding band on it. "Here's your key. First floor, about three doors down from here." He glanced between us one last time before he shuffled back off to his room.

With the large gold key on an oversized plastic keychain spouting the hotel's name, I took one of the bags off the floor and tossed it over my shoulder. It weighed significantly more than I was prepared for.

"Jesus, what do you have in here, a dead body?" I asked.

Malcolm grabbed the bag from off my shoulder and easily put it over his, picking the other off the ground as well. "I like to be prepared for anything. Sue me."

"Pfft. Like I could afford to sue anyone. I don't have a dime on me," I said.

He paused in the doorway, our bodies nearly touching. "Then you best not leave my side then, Mrs. Gavin."

I knew what he was saying. Don't be stupid. Don't try to run or be self-sacrificing.

"Would you spank me if I did, *Mr. Gavin?*" I couldn't help the flirtatious tone that escaped my lips. Malcolm didn't miss it either as he inhaled deeply. I'd made him uncomfortable. Good. Standing tall, I held up my left hand. "If we're gonna keep up this married act, I'm gonna need a ring. A big one." I winked.

"Right. We should come up with a story. Let's get some rest for now. Long day tomorrow."

I bowed my head and let him pass. I couldn't help but admire the view. The man had an impressive build. I had to give him that. And he was strong. Those bags were not light. It made me curious about what the hell was in there. And how unfazed I'd be if it *did* turn out to be a dead body. Nothing was going to surprise me anymore. Except maybe what spending the night in the same room with Malcolm would be like.

MALCOLM

The hotel room was just as horrific as I imagined it would be. The walls were covered in floor-to-ceiling fake wood paneling, on which hung several attempts at art. The lighting was a lovely flickering fluorescent, while the floors looked like puke. The yellow and brown shag rug in front of the door was threadbare at the entrance and likely hadn't seen a vacuum in months.

"Yeah, you're not sleeping on that carpet," Amanda said.

She was sitting on the "king" bed that was a queen at best.

"There's plenty of room here. And I don't bite. Well, I do, but I'll try and keep my hands to myself." She flashed her perfect smile at me, but I looked away.

Her flirtation was not directed at me. It was her default setting around men. "Amanda, you don't need to do that, you know." I placed the bags on the bed beside her.

"I'm not letting you sleep on that carpet—"

"No. Not that. The sexual innuendos. You don't have to do that with me. You don't need to flirt with me to ensure your safety. I'm not going to hurt you."

I studied her face as she took in my words. She obviously wasn't used to someone treating her with respect. Given her past relationship with men, it wasn't hard to understand why. She needed to know, however, that I wasn't like them. And the only way to convey that was to keep my hands off her. No matter how much I might want to push her down on that bed and— *No. Malcolm. She's not an object. You're here to help her. Nothing more.*

"I'm sorry," Amanda said. "Force of habit. I guess I'm just used to men wanting something from me."

"The only thing I want is for you to be as far away from Connor Brooks as we can get you."

She studied me for a moment as though she was deciding if I could be trusted or not. Gnawing on her lip, she cocked her head. "And once I'm safe, then we'll talk about how to save the other women?"

I nodded. "Yes. I promise. I'll find a way to get them out too. But only once I have you safe. Deal?" I held out my hand to shake hers.

She looked at my outstretched hand almost as though she were debating with herself if she could take me at my word.

"Amanda, I know believing I won't hurt you is a tall order. Not only am I virtually a stranger, but I'm a man. And I know in your life men have not been all that reliable. All I'm asking is for two days to get you to my safehouse."

"And then you'll ask me for sex?" Amanda smirked.

I frowned at her.

"I was kidding, calm down." She laughed, but there was an edge to it. "Seeing as how I don't have a ton of other options." She held out her hand for me to shake.

Our hands met as we shook, and I tried hard to ignore the shiver that went down my spine from her touch. She ran her thumb inside the palm of my hand.

"You have big hands."

"I do."

"You know what that means, don't you?" She smiled as her eyes darted unmistakably to my crotch.

"No. What does it mean?" I challenged.

"Big hands, large...gloves." She pulled her hand away and

backed herself over to the bed, grinning the whole time. She had never been more beautiful.

"So, what's really in these bags?" She tapped one of them with her foot.

"See for yourself." I walked over to her and unzipped the bag she'd kicked, so she could see inside. Her eyes nearly fell out of her head.

"Holy shit!" She dropped to her knees and pulled out two large wads of money. "Is this all filled with money?"

"And passports, foreign currency, legal documents, burner phones...that sort of thing."

"And what's in the other one? Gold bricks?" she shrieked.

"Nothing quite so grand. Clothing, hair dye, scissors, protein bars, medicine, and a first aid kit. Basic vanishing essentials."

"Jesus, you *are* prepared. Do you use these often?"

I sighed and sat on the edge of the bed. "I use them frequently enough to know what to put in a go-bag."

"A 'go-bag.'" She snickered, then stood up. "That's oddly hot." At that, she flinched. "Sorry. Jesus, I can't stop flirting with you."

I wanted to reach out and comfort her but that wasn't my place. Instead, I offered her the next best thing. "Why don't you grab the shower first? I'm going to map out our route for tomorrow. I want to throw in some side roads to make sure we aren't being followed. Might take us a little longer, but we've got nothing but time."

"You don't have to ask me twice. A hot shower sounds amazing. With actual soap to boot."

"He didn't give you soap?" I seethed.

"He barely let us shower. Unless he was the one doing the bathing. He doesn't trust us with anything that isn't bolted down. Literally. There is nothing in those cages that could be used to hurt him or ourselves."

My hands balled into fists. "Did he hurt you? Physically?"

Amanda gnawed at the bottom of her lip. "Nothing I couldn't

handle. But the other girls...they got it worse. Especially if I didn't listen to him."

"Why would it be worse for them if you didn't listen?" I was thoroughly confused. She shrugged.

"Because instead of hurting me for not obeying, he'd beat them. Fastest way to make us comply. Connor knew we'd be sympathetic. Which is why we need to make sure to save them. When he finds out you stole me... He'll take it out on them."

My blood was boiling, imagining the hell she must have endured. The favors she must have granted to protect herself or the others. "I'll find a way to make him pay for everything he's done to you."

She ran her fingers up her arm as though holding herself. "Yeah, well now you know why I was willing to go back to him. If I could save even one of them..."

"Even if it meant risking your own life?"

"Absolutely," she said without hesitation. "I'm expendable. No one would miss me if I were gone."

"I would," I said. I was surprised by how honest that answer was. "Which is why you can't go back now. I'd miss you too much." I walked over to her and placed a hand on her shoulder. She flinched slightly. "Promise me, Amanda. Promise you won't try to go back there. I'll find a way to save those girls, but I refuse to sacrifice you to do it. I need you to trust me."

"Trust?" She raised her eyebrows. "No offense, but that's the word every man who has ever hurt me has used."

Her words gutted me in a way I wasn't prepared for. While I knew she held no shred of deception when she confessed that, however, convincing her I wasn't like them would be one of the hardest things I'd ever have to do.

"You're right," I said. "I'm sorry. I can't ask you to trust me. That needs to be earned. So that's what I'm going to do, Amanda. From this moment on. I'm going to do whatever I can to earn your trust. However long that takes. Okay?"

Her eyes met mine for a moment, and I swear tears were there, but she gave me a nod before heading into the bathroom to take her shower.

Satisfied she wasn't going to try to escape out the bathroom window, I took that time to go through the bags. Snatching the first one from off the floor, I tossed it onto the bed and pulled out a few paper maps. I didn't trust using the car's GPS. I wasn't sure how sophisticated 'Connor's tracking skills were. Travel was a big part of my job, so reading maps and road signs was not unfamiliar to me.

I wasn't looking for the fastest route, I was searching for the off-the-beaten paths Connor, or his men, might not think to look.

From my suit jacket pocket, I pulled out a small notepad. I flipped open the metal casing around it that had my initials engraved in it. My real initials. DL. I ran the pad of my thumb over the cursive. My mom gave this to me on my seventeenth birthday. She was a bit of a note-taker herself. She was always jotting things down. She passed that trait onto me. I've used this same notepad holder ever since. Every time I take it out, I think of her and how happy she'd been to give me such a fancy gift. Money was always tight, but she'd found the case at a thrift store and paid to have it engraved.

Looking at the map, there were two choices. After we got off I-90 we'd either take I-94 or I-82. The latter would take about an hour longer.

In the notebook, I jotted down: I-90 E, I-82 E, I-84 E, I-80 E, then hop onto I-90 E.

Closing the pad, I slipped it back into my jacket and refolded the map, tossing it back in the bag. The map landed on one of the burner phones. I debated calling to check in but that wasn't protocol. Twenty-four hours. Minimum. Darcy and Camila needed time to align their alibis. Not to mention their hands would be full closing up the house. So far so good. Even with the extra travel time, everything should be buttoned up within a few days. So far so good.

Don't stop now. Keep reading with your copy of THE SAFEHOUSE today!

And don't miss more from Danielle Bannister. Stay up to date on all of her release information, cover reveals, sales, and giveaways by joining her newsletter.

Don't miss the continuation of *The Captive* series with THE SAFEHOUSE, available now, and be sure to sign-up to receive all the news and updates from Danielle Bannister.

He wanted his property back...

Amanda Jackson had succumbed to the fact that she'd been a captive. That she'd involuntary fallen victim to an underground market of despicable men. To protect herself, she was willing to try anything. Even attempting to convince her captor that he loved her. That plan backfired.

Connor Brooks didn't show emotions with his captives. Bring them in, get them out, collect the cash, and repeat the process. Amanda, however, was different. He found himself growing attached to her. Possessive. When another man stole him from her, Connor was determined to get her back. By any means necessary.

Malcolm Luxx was used to dealing with shady business practices. He ran one of his own in the art world. He drew the line at Connor's business. When he discovered one of the women he'd taken was his high school crush, he swooped in and saved her. Or so he thought.

Will the safehouse Malcolm has across the country be far enough to keep Connor and his goons from finding Amanda? Or by taking Amanda, has Malcolm just signed both of their death certificates?

He wanted his property back. And he'd get her even in The Safehouse.

Please sign up for the City Owl Press newsletter for chances to win special subscriber-only contests and giveaways as well as receiving information on upcoming releases and special excerpts.

All reviews are **welcome** and **appreciated**. Please consider leaving one on your favorite social media and book buying sites.

Escape Your World. Get Lost in Ours! www.cityowlpress.com

ACKNOWLEDGMENTS

Thank you to my beta readers Cassy Bunnell, Angela Domenichelli, Julie Cassar, and Danielle DeVor, who helped turn some of these rough ideas into something solid. As you can imagine, this subject was a difficult one to navigate. Your honesty and suggestions help round out this story and these characters in ways I wouldn't have been able to on my own.

Also, thanks to City Owl Press for always having the courage to push story boundaries for the sake of solid storytelling. They believe in my writing, even when I don't.

ABOUT THE AUTHOR

DANIELLE BANNISTER lives with her two children in Mid-Coast Maine, along with her precious coffee pot and peppermint mocha creamer. She holds a BA in Theater from the University of Southern Maine and her Masters in Literary Education from the University of Orono.

When she's not on the stage or on the page, you'll find her drinking tea and binge-watching all the Netflix. As one does.

www.daniellebannister.com

facebook.com/BannisterBooks
x.com/dbannisterbooks
instagram.com/daniellebannisterbooks
pinterest.com/bannisterbooks
bookbub.com/authors/danielle-bannister
tiktok.com/@daniellebannisterbooks

ABOUT THE PUBLISHER

City Owl Press is a cutting edge indie publishing company, bringing the world of romance and speculative fiction to discerning readers.

Escape Your World. Get Lost in Ours!

www.cityowlpress.com

facebook.com/YourCityOwlPress

x.com/cityowlpress

instagram.com/cityowlbooks

pinterest.com/cityowlpress